Praise for WIND

"*WIND* is exciting, uplifting, inspiring, educational, and has so much depth and messages for children and adults alike!"

—EIMEAR STASSIN, Soul Based Life Coach

"This book is an allegory for our times."

—LINDA STEWART, PhD, LMFT, Grandmother, USA

"This is a gift. I see it made into an animated screenplay."

—PATRISHA CLARKIN, Grove Tender for Tree Sisters, Canada

"*WIND* is classic fantasy."

—SHEILA WILLIAMSON, Meditator and Gardener, UK

"*WIND* is insightful, engaging, delightful, moving, inspiring, truth-telling, relieving, and evocative."

—JENNY ROSE SMITH, Deep Listening Guide, UK

"I am enjoying this book as I would a cup of tea, sipping slowly and enjoying immensely."

—BEVERLY TEMPLETON,
Co-founder of Global Tree Lovers Website.

"Davidson delivers an entertaining story with a forward-moving balance of action and dialogue The latter often includes words of wisdom such as 'Each day is a gift' to complement the idea of an interconnected ecosystem and the sentiment that if humans learn to heal themselves, they'll also heal the earth."

—*BLUEINK REVIEWS*

"The crispiness of the writing, the unforgettable characters, and the cunning plot will have readers racing through the pages of this book. Ellen Dee Davidson melds the art of descriptive prose with the quirkiness in character and exciting dialogues to touch the hearts of readers in unexpected ways. It is, simply put, a lovely adventure with a delightful end."

—*THE BOOK COMMENTARY*

"Imagine a children's fiction book which conveys environmental values, connecting from the heart and bringing forth a more liveable world in a 'can't put it down' 'action packed' novel. *WIND,* by Ellen Dee Davidson, is such a book. Important environmental topics such as soil health, mycelium and nutrient transfer between trees, biodiversity, and ancient understandings of the importance of elements that are in all living creatures are woven by magic and enchantment with the values of non-judgement, acceptance and love of others and belief in Self. *WIND* provides a lively story that can complement environmental literacy—the magic with the facts. … The magic in *WIND* is very different from Harry Potter magic. It is magic that we can possibly all do, if we dare to dream and wake up."

—MERRILEE BAKER,
Nurse and Environmental Educator, Australia

"Imagine a world where trees are wise helpers, where animals can guide us to safety, where stories are gathered and remembered by the guardian of the deep sea, where greed and hatred become a place where everything turns to poison, where befriending the stranger becomes the path to fulfilling wishes and dreams. Welcome to the world of *WIND.*"

—ELYSE POMERANZ, Waldorf Educator and Mentor, Canada

"From evolving friendships to influences that lead to self-doubt, Davidson crafts a story filled not just with action, but insights: *'I was here for long enough to realize the Poison One couldn't stand a true friendship like ours—the kind that can accept each other exactly as we are.' 'And ourselves too,' added Katie.'* … *WIND* holds an important message for middle-grade readers, couched in the guise of an adventure that adds food for thought about connections, support systems, courage, and the power of believing in oneself and the world."

—DIANE DONOVAN, Senior Reviewer, *Midwest Book Review*

"Fueled by young Katie's desire to heal her parents' struggles at home, we are reminded of the unquestionable love and support we received from Earth as children. Each character in *WIND* comes to life, guiding us to restore the missing truth, whose absence is currently poisoning our world. Ultimately awakening an undeniable sense of hope and possibilities, intelligently weaving both the metaphysical and scientific, *WIND* offers a new expanded way to relate to and support each and every conscious living being in our world."

—KATHLEEN BRIGIDINA,
TreeSisters Community Engagement Coordinator and Artist Liaison

"Vividly imagined and lyrically told, *WIND* holds drama and adventure, as well as numerous beautiful descriptive passages while Katie is on her quest. … YA readers will enjoy following her and her companion, the boastful Za, as they make their way through the perils and enchantments that beset their quest."

—*BOOKLIFE PRIZE*

"Overall, the whole story is well-written and magical from the beginning until the end. It was a fun and amazing read! Well done!"

—CLOIE BELLE DAFFON, *Readers' Favorites*

"A magical adventure with ecological undertones, Katie is whisked to another realm where she must save it from The Poison One."

—*REEDSY REVIEWS*

"This story helps us remember what is true."

—ELYSE POMERANZ,
Waldorf Educator and Mentor

"Davidson shares her passion for fantasy and the environment in this vibrant novel. … Love for nature shines as the author's overarching message. … An excellent scene showing the connection between trees and fungi gives adventure fans a topic for further study. Also noteworthy is that Katie and Za could not look more different, but they win by embracing their similarities."

—*KIRKUS REVIEWS*

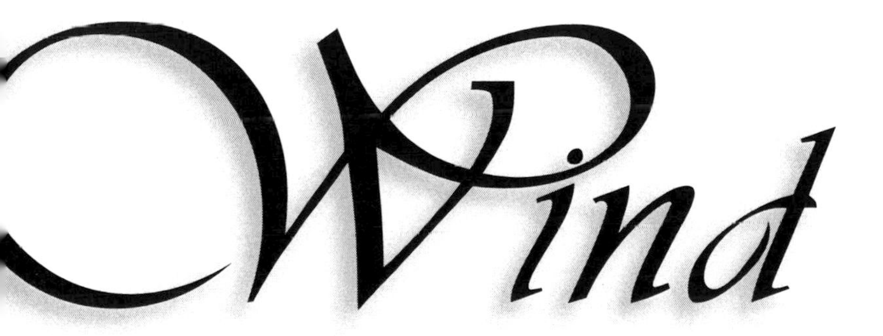

Ellen Dee Davidson

WIND

Printed in the United States of America

Cover illustration by Carolan Raleigh-Hawes
Graphic design by Claire Flint Last

Luminare Press
442 Charnelton St.
Eugene, OR 97401
www.luminarepress.com

LCCN: 2021914791
ISBN: 978-1-64388-718-0

For Stevie Alanna

Table of Contents

CHAPTER ONE

Shaken Up

Katie tugged on her brown braid as she stared out the window, noticing the green leaves on the oak tree swaying in the breeze. She let her mind wander as Mr. Pinski's voice washed over her, talking about the latest chapter in their life science book. She couldn't concentrate. Not with everything going on at home.

"Will you listen to me?"

Startled, Katie looked around. But it wasn't Mr. Pinski. He was up at the front of the class, looking crisp and professional in his blue button-down shirt as he spoke about the importance of biodiversity and of earthworms to the soil. Most of her classmates were listening, or at least pretending to listen. Julian doodled and Maggie passed a note to Leila, probably about Maggie's coming birthday party. No one was talking. Mr. Pinski wouldn't put up with that when he was giving a lecture. She stared back out the window.

"Will you listen to me?" the rough creaky voice asked again and a few branches on the oak tree shook, almost as if the tree were waving an arm at her.

'Who wants me to listen?' Katie thought, confused. 'Who's talking?'

"Me! Outside." A twig on the oak rubbed slowly against the window and swallows darted up into the air.

Katie stared at the tree. 'You can talk? And I hear you in my head?'

"If you listen," answered the odd voice. It sounded almost like two branches rubbing together, shush-squeak-creak-shush, but the words in her mind were clear. "I've been having a hard time finding anyone who will." Oak branches waved in a nonexistent wind, making a sort of distressed moaning sound. "No one seems to notice me and I need help!" Leaves rustled together with a crackle, crunch, swish, sniff-sniff, like someone crying. Katie couldn't help feeling sad for the tree; the oak seemed so desperate.

'I guess I'm hearing you now,' Katie thought slowly, wondering if it was true, wondering if hearing a tree in her mind was even possible, and then remembering how sometimes in the past she'd almost felt like the plants in Dad's garden talked to her, asking her for more water, or telling her how delicious the sunlight felt on their leaves. Maybe it was possible. 'How can I help you?'

"My branches," sighed the oak. "Please, no more pruning. I'm losing too much vital force. Promise to…tell…them to stop cut…" The tree's leaves dangled limply, looking sad and weary.

'I will,' Katie thought back.

"Ahem!" Mr. Pinski cleared his throat. He was standing right in front of her desk. "Are you with us today Katie?"

Katie took in a breath. "Yes. But I have to tell you," she blurted, "The oak outside the window doesn't want any more of her branches trimmed."

Mr. Pinski's blue eyes widened. "Sounds like you were having quite a daydream!"

"No! It wasn't a daydream. I heard her clearly." Katie continued, determined to share the oak's message. "She says it's using too much of her vital force and she…"

Giggles burst out of Maggie. Then Tessa started laughing too, and soon the whole class was cracking up. They laughed hard for a few seconds and then Mr. Pinski held up his hand in the signal for quiet and the class settled back down, although Katie could still hear a few suppressed snorts and an escaped giggle. Out of the corner of her eye, Katie saw Maggie make the cuckoo sign, circling her ear with one finger, and whisper to Leila, "I'm not inviting her." She paused for a second, and then added in a clear carrying whisper, "Or Amy. Must be as crazy as Katie to hang out with her."

Katie's cheeks warmed with embarrassment, but she held her head up and kept her promise to the tree, "She really doesn't want any more branches cut." Katie gave Mr. Pinski a pleading look. "Will you tell the office or the grounds keeper, or whoever you're supposed to tell?"

Mr. Pinski replied, "You have one of the best imaginations in the 6th grade, Katie. Perhaps you can put it to use in creative writing? Right now, we've got to get back to the life cycle of earthworms. If you did your homework, you should be able to tell me if an earthworm begins with a live birth or an egg?"

He waited expectantly and Katie answered, "An egg." She *had* done her homework. "When they are fertilized the eggs stay in a cocoon until the baby worms hatch and burrow down into the earth."

Mr. Pinksi smiled. "Good!" And then he turned back to the whiteboard and wrote, "What do earthworms eat?"

Katie tried to pay attention, but she just could not keep her mind on what Mr. Pinski was saying. She'd completely failed the oak tree. 'I'm sorry,' she thought towards the tree, but this time there was no reply. The tree's branches drooped

Finally the bell rang and students burst out the door into the late August sunshine. Katie picked up her small blue backpack and joined Amy at the classroom door. Most of the kids took the bus or had their parents pick them up, but she and Amy loved to walk home together. It was only a mile and went past the red brick library, a mini-mall with a grocery store, and a block of houses. Some of the homes were a bit run down with peeling paint. Others were tidy. One even had a white picket fence. The golden retriever behind it barked at them and Amy called, "It's okay, Toby. It's just us." Then they turned onto their own street. More rural here, the ranch style homes were separated by a few acres. They passed several oaks and Katie felt a twinge. "I don't think Mr. Pinski believed me."

"Why did you do that?" asked Amy, running her fingers through her slightly frizzy red hair.

Katie kicked a pebble, feeling bad that now the oak tree's message wouldn't be delivered. "I had to. The oak…" She stopped in front of her driveway.

Amy pursed her lips together for a moment before saying, "The other kids think you're nuts, and they are starting to think I'm nuts too for hanging out with you. Did you hear Maggie whisper to Leila?"

Katie nodded unhappily. "I'm sorry, Amy. I wanted to go to that party too." Maggie always had the best birthday parties. "Do you want to come in? Mom made cookies."

"Sure," said Amy, following her up the wooden porch steps and into the green ranch style house.

Katie stopped in the kitchen long enough to grab two glasses of milk and a plate of chocolate chip cookies before walking down the hall to her bedroom. The two of them dumped their packs on the wooden desk and sat on the white shag rug. Amy stuffed half a cookie into her mouth.

Sasha meowed. Katie stared at her ginger colored cat. Sasha paced back and forth and then jumped onto the window sill. "Amy, Sasha's trying to tell me something."

Amy swallowed the cookie, took a sip of milk, and then gave Katie a disbelieving look. "You're talking to the cat now, too?"

Katie shrugged. "Sort of."

Amy glanced at the cat on the windowsill before shaking her head. "Your cat looks fine to me."

Sasha meowed again and the word "Earth!" rang crystal clear in Katie's head.

"She says something's wrong," insisted Katie, "with the earth."

Amy exhaled. "Look, Katie, I don't mind if you want to pretend you can talk to trees and cats when we're alone, but you really embarrassed me at school."

Katie looked a little hopelessly into Amy's green eyes. If she couldn't even get Amy to believe her, then it was a sure thing no one else would. "I wasn't pretending then, and I'm not pretending now."

Sasha arched her back and hissed. "The cat really is warning us," Katie said, "I just don't understand about what."

Amy glanced briefly at Sasha, shaking her red hair out of her eyes. "Maybe she's upset because your parents have been fighting?"

Katie nodded. "Maybe. It's getting worse," said Katie, flashing back to the fight. '*You're full of impossible dreams,' Mom had said, glaring at Dad. 'You just want to grow your forest garden to save the world. But let me tell you,' she paused for breath before continuing in that tone she got sometimes when she just couldn't take it all anymore, 'My salary as a music teacher is not enough to support the three of us.'*

Amy passed Katie the cookie plate. "Anybody home?"

Katie sighed heavily. "I was just remembering the big fight we had. Mom was so mad she yelled at me," Katie said and then imitated her Mom's voice, "Katie Consuela Rosa Noriega, you are a rude ungrateful girl." Katie shook her head. "You know she's mad when she uses all my names like that."

"At least you have lots of pretty names," Amy said, reaching out and squeezing Katie's brown hand with her freckled white fingers. "I wish I had a flower name. I'm just Amy Scott."

"Dad told me a bunch of names is a part of our Mexican heritage. Rosa is for his Irish half, although he says in Ireland it'd be Rose." Katie gave a half-smile. "Mom named me Katie after her grandmother, but Dad always calls me Rosa. Says I'm his most precious rose, but that was before." Katie felt her face crumple. She probably wasn't his precious rose anymore.

"I'm sorry about the fight," Amy said.

"It was bad, Amy," Katie confessed. "Even I got into this one. By the end, all three of us were screaming at each other."

Amy gave her a sympathetic look and waited for Katie to say more.

Katie blinked back a tear and told Amy the part she didn't want to say. "They're talking divorce."

The room was silent for a long heartbeat. Finally, Amy said, "It's not so bad—once you get used to two houses. At first, I was always leaving my homework in the wrong house."

Katie knew her friend was trying to comfort her, but she didn't want her parents to get divorced. Why couldn't they all be happy together? Why couldn't Dad get a regular job? Then, maybe, they could keep the house. Three acres was big enough for her to have a horse if she could ever convince her parents.

"Hurry!" Sasha urged mentally, interrupting Katie's thoughts.

Katie frowned at her cat. Why was Sasha so upset?

Amy sighed. "I wish I didn't have to go, but it's almost four and you know how my mom gets when I'm late."

Katie nodded in understanding.

"I'll call you tonight, okay?" asked Amy, gathering her school pack.

"Sounds good," said Katie, a bit distracted by Sasha.

"Ok. Bye," said Amy.

"Adios," replied Katie, going to the window and picking Sasha up. The cat's fur stood up straight, like porcupine quills. "What's wrong, Sash?"

NOTHING STIRRED OUTSIDE. IT WAS TOO QUIET. THE birds in the rhododendron bush stopped singing. Katie listened to the shsh shsh of tree leaves rubbing together, then shut the window firmly. "Meeeow!"

Katie held the cat close. "Do you want to go outside?"

Sasha unsheathed her claws into Katie's arms.

"Ouch!" Katie dropped the cat.

"Outside!" the cat shouted in her mind. "Now!"

The glass in the window rattled and the floor rolled beneath Katie, like a ship. As books crashed off shelves, Katie staggered to her bedroom doorway, fighting to stay on her feet.

The paper mache globe swung crazily on its string. The fairy on her shelf cracked as it hit the desk, throwing shards of pink glass. One grazed Katie's arm and blood oozed out of the cut.

Katie's heart thrummed in her ears. An alarm clock tumbled off the bedside table. Suddenly the rumbling stopped. *Was the earthquake over? Was it safe for her to leave the doorway?* Dimly, Katie recalled something about aftershocks and moving outside slowly. She squeezed her fingers into sweating palms, longing to get out of the house, to find the neighbors, to get help.

Sasha streaked by, a blur of ginger. Katie couldn't help herself. She raced after Sasha, desperate to get out of the house. Her tennis shoes slapped the wood floor of the hall. A hole gaped in the center of the floor. She swerved just in time.

Katie steadied herself against the wall, inhaling the damp cold air that rose from the basement. *Mom, come home. COME HOME.* She pictured her mom with stray strands of curly brown hair tangled in her glasses. If only she could will her mom here. Creeping around the edge of the fissure, Katie was just in time to see Sasha shoot the rest of the way down the hall and out the cat door.

Without warning, the earth heaved and Katie fell straight into the crack.

CHAPTER TWO

The Orb

Katie landed with a thud, her hand slamming against something hard. Pain beat a steady rhythm against her skull. Thoughts floated slowly through her head. *What happened*?

She opened her eyes wide. Jagged shapes slowly came into focus, shadows against the black. There was something familiar about those shapes. Katie willed her scattered thoughts to come together, to make sense. *Of course! Dad's tools.* She must have fallen into the basement. Damp seeped into her pants. Her hand rubbed against slime. The floor was wet. *Must be from the leaking water heater.* She'd have to tell Dad it was leaking again.

Sweat beaded Katie's brow as she forced her stiff legs to move. She released her breath. *Good. Nothing broken*. She'd need to be in one piece to pull herself back out of the crack.

No point looking for the door. It was always padlocked from the outside. Child-proofed, Mom said. Katie strained her eyes, searching for the crack. She shook so hard her teeth rattled. If an aftershock closed the crack… Katie stopped herself from imagining more, although she couldn't stop her racing heart. She had to get out, get help.

"Mom!" she shrieked. Then she realized there was no way Mom could have made it back from the lawyer this fast.

"Shh!" a voice came from somewhere in the dark.

"Who's there?" Katie asked, startled.

There was no answer. Across the room a dim light winked. Katie sat up, ignoring the sharp throb in the back of her head. Too dizzy and stunned to stand, Katie crawled towards the light.

Something soft and sticky slid across her hand. "Yuck!" screamed Katie, flinging it away.

"Would you be quiet!" said a low, gravelly voice, and now Katie saw a face, eerily illuminated in the pale light. The thick gloom made the face look like it floated across the room without a body.

She rubbed her eyes. "I'm hallucinating."

"You're not," said the deep voice.

"This doesn't make sense," said Katie, gingerly touching the lump on the back of her head. "H-h-how did you get in my basement?"

It was hard to see the figure in the small flickering light. As far as Katie could tell, the person was short and wore a jumpsuit. "Who are you?" she asked, feeling relieved that at least there was someone with her.

"Za."

"Za? That's an unusual name," said Katie.

"Just be quiet so I can set my orb," replied Za, not even bothering to ask if she had a name.

"I'm Katie," she told him anyway, adding, "What's an orb?"

Za held up a grapefruit-sized object. A faint light pulsed from it—the only light in the room.

"Oh, good," said Katie. "We can use your light to find our way out of here."

Za fiddled with the protruding metal knobs. "Shh! I'm adjusting the coordinates."

"Coordinates? For a flashlight?"

Za didn't say anything. He just gave Katie a disgusted look. His eyes seemed yellow in the underground light. "Give me your light and I'll look for the hole," said Katie, reaching for the orb. "It has to be close to where I fell through."

Za jerked his orb away and barked, "Don't touch!"

As the light came close to his face, Katie saw him clearly for the first time.

She dropped her hand and backed away. Purple skin, yellow eyes, blue hair and blue teeth. His bare feet had long gnarly toes that gripped the rocks like the roots of a tree. No one looked like that.

"Dad! Help!" yelled Katie. But Dad had stormed out that morning and she knew he wouldn't be home any time soon.

"Be quiet before I have to do something to make you shut-up!" growled Za.

Katie hurried away from him as fast as she could, stumbling over the slippery rubble. When she was far enough away that Za's light was only a pinpoint, she collapsed into a tight, protective ball. Her stomach formed a hard lump in the center of that ball. The sound of Za's heavy breathing carried through the pitch black room. *The basement was always padlocked...how did he get in here?*

No time to figure that out. She had to get out of here now. She looked up, searching for the crack. It should be lighter... She'd fallen during the day, after all. But she couldn't see a thing except for the candle-like glow from Za's orb. She half-walked, half-crawled, groping her way along the wall. It was uneven and rough. Something sharp cut her palm. Katie flinched from the pain and wiped her bleeding hand on her pants. Another one of those sticky wet bug things plopped on Katie's neck. "Ick!"

“Darn!” shouted Za. “I almost had it.”

Katie forced herself to stand, to walk back to Za. He had the only light in the room. Without that light, she’d never find a way out of the basement. “I’m sorry,” she said, “but if you’ll just share your light, I know I can find the way out of here.”

“My orb is the only way out of here,” stated Za. “Otherwise, we’ll end up trapped between.”

“You mean trapped under,” Katie corrected. “We’re under my house and if there’s an aftershock, we might really be trapped.”

Za frowned. “If you’ll stop chattering, I’ll set the orb and get us both back where we belong. Every time you speak it causes interference, and this is an extremely sensitive instrument.”

“Please,” begged Katie, tears running down her face. “Just share your light.”

Za didn’t seem to hear her. He watched the orb. It began to hum, glowing brighter. The humming grew louder. “It’s not supposed to do this!” moaned Za.

The orb expanded, pulsing and flashing bright light. Then it exploded in a shower of sparks. “No!” shrieked Za.

The light was so fierce that, for an instant, Katie could see everything. Spiky rocks towered over them. Rubble coated in green slime was all around her tennis shoes. This wasn’t her basement. Where was she?

CHAPTER THREE

Stuck Between

Za's sobs faded, leaving only the bone chilling quiet. "Are you okay?" asked Katie, wishing she could see him. "Are you hurt?"

"Of course I'm hurt!"

"What happened? Did you get burned?"

"No, I didn't get burned. I'm not *physically* hurt. This is worse."

Katie's heart pounded. "What's worse?"

"You're what's worse," Za accused. "If you hadn't made such a racket, I could have concentrated on my orb, and it wouldn't have shattered."

"It's not my fault," declared Katie. "I didn't cause an earthquake and I didn't make your orb shatter. You're the one who..." but Katie didn't know how to finish. She had no idea why the orb had exploded or what, if anything, Za had done wrong. "Oh, never mind. It doesn't matter now, anyway," she cried miserably. "Nothing is making any sense: the crack in the ceiling is gone, I'm stuck here with a...a..." And what could she call Za? When his orb had exploded, she'd seen in the burst of light that he was short, the height of a five year old, but knew from the way he spoke Za was obviously much older. His body was shaped oddly too, with skinny legs and squat broad shoulders, like some sort of gnome from a fairy tale. And he had those outsized feet! "I don't understand who you are or where all these rocks came from. I don't understand why I'm not in my basement."

"We're stuck between," Za said.

"Between?" repeated Katie. "Between what?"

Za's breath hissed out in an exasperated sigh. "My guardian warned me about getting trapped between," he said quietly, "but, of course, I never thought it'd happen to me."

"What are you talking about? Are you crazy?" She took a step back, losing her balance on the uneven ground. She put her hand down to steady herself. It brushed against something soft and smooth, like plastic.

"I told you before—when you kept interrupting me while I was trying to set the coordinates. We never were in your basement." Za gave a disgusted grunt. "Now even I don't know where we are. According to my guardian, between can be almost anywhere."

Katie's mouth went dry. "What on Earth are you talking about?"

Za laughed—a sharp sound that bounced off the rocks. "Earth? Is that where you're from? No wonder you have those ridiculous brown eyes and are so ignorant. Your planet is practically quarantined. We learn about it in school as an example of how things can go wrong. Some people even get special permits to go there to study the planetary effects of living out of balance. You Earth people have completely lost your feet on the ground. My teachers taught us that life on Earth may not even survive and you'll have an uninhabitable planet."

"Quit it!" Katie said. "This is no time for jokes. There's no way you're going to convince me you're not from Earth."

"I have two worlds," said Za matter-of-factly. His voice sounded close, even though she couldn't see him. *What was he doing, moving around in the dark*?

Clunk, clunk, thud.

"What's that?" asked Katie.

Za snorted. "Don't get so wound up. It's only me. Anyway, like I was saying, I was on my way from Mother's world to visit Father on Stella when something blew me off course."

"Let me get this straight," Katie said sarcastically. "You're a lost alien from two planets who just happens to speak English."

"I can speak anything." Za's voice carried proudly over the sound of the stones he jiggled. "My guardian gave me the gift of tongues for my last birthday so I automatically use the same language as anyone speaking to me."

Katie's stomach cramped. She'd never seen anything like Za's orb or the serrated rocks all around them, which looked like sharp, pointed teeth. And Za certainly didn't look like other people. She had a sickening feeling that what he said might be true. *Could he really be an alien? Could she really be on another world?*

Something grabbed Katie's ankle.

"Aaagh!" she shrieked.

"Calm down," ordered Za. "It's only me. I got your leg by mistake."

Katie shivered. It gave her the creeps to think he was close enough to touch her and she couldn't even see him. "I wish we had some light."

The black quiet was broken by the rustle of movement, the clatter of a dislodged stone, and the sound of footsteps leading away.

"Where are you going?" called Katie. "I can't see a thing."

"Just looking for a piece of my orb. Even a small shard could give us some light."

Katie picked up the smooth plastic thing she'd felt before. "Is this it?"

"How can I tell?" asked Za. "Even with my excellent night vision, it's so dark in here that I can't see very well. Try rubbing it between your palms."

Katie obeyed. The fragment grew warm, beginning to glow. Katie quit rubbing and held up the object, which gave off about the same amount of light as a match.

"Give it to me," said Za.

In the dim light, Katie saw his face. My God, he looked weird. She clutched the shard tighter. "No, I'll hold it."

"Listen, it's my orb. And, besides, I'm more competent than you are. Now, give it to me and I'll find another one for you."

"I'll hold it," Katie repeated stubbornly, "and we can look for another piece for *you*."

Za scowled. "Hold it lower," he ordered, rummaging around in the debris.

The small light revealed more of those slimy wet bugs crawling between the rocks. They were long with lots of legs, like centipedes. Normally Katie didn't mind bugs. Dad had taught her about the important place they had in the web of life. But right now, the sight of their hairy bodies gave her the creeps.

Za moved stone after stone, sorting carefully throughout the rubble. Katie's back felt sore from stooping over with the light, and her eyes ached.

"I don't think we're going to find another piece of my orb," Za said at last, "and we should try to discover the way out of here." He reached out his hand. "Give the light to me and I'll hold it so we can see enough to take one step at a time."

Katie gripped it tighter, shaking her head.

Za snatched the shard out of her hand.

Katie stuck out her tongue. "Pig!"

"What's a pig?" Za asked conversationally, beginning to pick his way around the rocks.

"Someone who hogs stuff—like you," Katie answered, thinking that pigs were intelligent animals and didn't deserve to be compared with this nincompoop. She didn't know whether to follow Za or not. It made more sense to stay right where she was until daylight tomorrow. Since Amy had left before 4 and it was already dark, she must have been knocked out by the fall and missed more time than she realized. That was the only explanation she could think of.

Za continued to walk away with the light. Katie scrambled after him. "Wait!" She took one careful step at a time, trying not to slip on the uneven rocks. A faint trickling sound broke the quiet. She struggled on in silence, grazing her arms against the smooth towers of stone. Nothing changed. Every step looked and felt the same as the one before.

Za slipped and dropped the light. Immediately the two of them were sunk back into the gloom.

Katie swallowed. If she'd carried the light, this wouldn't have happened. She'd have been more careful.

"This is pointless," grumbled Za. "I need to contact my guardian. He could get us out of here in a nanosecond."

"Well, why don't you?"

"I don't know the tunings. We don't learn them until after initiation."

As if that explained anything. Katie crouched down, doing her best to avoid the bugs. Za was so close that she could smell his sweet/sour alien odor—like an overripe apple going to vinegar—although she couldn't see him at all. Katie groped in the rock-pile, feeling for the smooth plastic shard carefully so she didn't grab another one of those bugs by accident. The piece of Za's orb had to be around here somewhere. Slime. Rock. Small moving body. And, at last, "I've got it!" she exclaimed, rubbing the smooth shape between her palms until it glowed.

"Thanks," said Za, reaching out his hand.

Katie pulled the piece of orb back. "I'll hold it. That way it won't get dropped."

"Fine," said Za in a disgusted tone that let Katie know he didn't think it was fine at all. "But I think we should try something else. We're not getting anywhere bumbling around. For all we know we could be going around in circles and, with your inferior Earth vision, you'll probably get hurt."

"My vision might not be as good as yours," said Katie, "but at least I'm not rude and insulting." Katie swallowed around the sudden lump that grew in her throat. *I was rude to my parents.* Her tongue felt fat and dry and her mouth was full of a metallic taste.

Katie walked gingerly, picking her way through the rubble. Za followed her so closely that she felt his breath on the back of her neck. She rubbed her dry tongue over cracked lips, wishing for something to drink. Her thirst almost took her mind off of the horrible fear. Maybe that faint plink-plink sound was water. Katie stopped every few steps to listen. The plink-plink turned into a splish-splash. Sure sounded like water. They rounded a bend and found a tiny stream cascading down the sheer rocks. She sniffed. *Smells like water.* She scooped a little in her palm and cautiously tasted it. Za put his long tongue straight into the running water and lapped it up, like a dog.

Katie carefully set the glowing shard down and cupped her palms. She drank and drank, until water sloshed around in her stomach. Then she sat back on her heels and watched the water bubble over the rocks. It disappeared in the blackness beyond the small area of light shed by the fragment. Dad always told her that the thing to do if she was ever lost and found a river or creek was to follow it downstream. He said that eventually that would lead her to some sort of civilization. "Let's follow the water," Katie said, reaching for the shard.

Za grabbed it first.

"Don't drop it this time."

"Don't worry," Za replied. "I never make the same mistake twice." He grinned, revealing his repulsive blue teeth. "Your idea of following the stream is good. At least we will have plenty to drink, which I prefer, even if I can live for two weeks without water."

"Yeah," agreed Katie, but she hoped they didn't get sick. Dad always purified the water when he took her backpacking, and she certainly didn't have anything to purify it with here: no water filter, way to boil it, or iodine pills.

Za stood up, grabbing the shard. He held the light in front of them. Katie followed him slowly over the slippery, uneven rocks. *The stream has to lead somewhere,* she told herself. *It has to.*

CHAPTER FOUR

A Mysterious Woman

A draft of cold moist air slicked against Katie's face. The orb light dimmed and fluttered out. Instead of plunging them back into the impenetrable shadows, a hazy light now drifted in from around a bend. Katie craned her neck back, expecting to see sky. But the vertical rocks continued overhead, forming an arched roof. "We're in a cave!"

"The Cave of Forgetting," answered a melodious voice. Not Za's annoying tone. Katie's head whipped around, eyes squinting, straining to see. A woman emerged in the half-light. She clicked her fingers and a lion nuzzled against her heels.

Za inhaled with a sharp hiss. "Wh-what is that beast? Is it dangerous?"

The woman shrugged. "That depends."

"Who are you?" whispered Katie.

The woman laughed, a musical sound, like wind rustling past leaves. "Now that is a difficult question. I appear in many forms with many names in many lands, but you may call me Dania. It is enough that I am the one who heard your call."

"But we didn't call," said Katie, confused.

"A heart in fear always calls," said the woman, beckoning with her arm. "Come. We dare not remain here too long." She turned and began to walk away. Za followed close behind her.

"Wait!" cried Katie. "I have to stay near here so that I can find the crack and get back home."

Dania turned. "If you remain in the Cave of Forgetting, you will soon forget everyone you've ever known. You may even forget yourself!" Dania gestured for them to follow. "Come," she repeated. "Your only hope of returning home lies somewhere else."

Katie stalled, afraid to leave. How could she get home if she left the area where she fell through? Dad said to stay put if she got lost. But he'd also told her to follow water downstream and it would usually lead her to some sort of civilization. *Which one was it?* Dad had never been lost on another world and never met someone like Dania. Katie sucked her cheeks in against her braces, thinking that she probably wouldn't survive long if she stayed here alone, then she hurried after Dania.

Light filtered in through an overhanging arch so that Katie could see Dania more clearly as the mysterious woman adjusted her green-gold head wrap. Katie squinted, but couldn't quite tell if the wrap was made out of cloth or leaves and branches. Whether it was cloth or leaves, the gold in the head wrap and matching dress complimented Dania's darker honey skin perfectly. She was absolutely beautiful. Dania stopped in front of a boulder blocking the narrow passage out, then she moved through; her body fitting itself to the opening like water flowing across a stream bed. The lion squeezed around with slightly more effort. Za kept his distance from the lion, motioning for Katie to go next. She shimmied through the tight passage. As soon as her eyes adjusted to the light, Katie took in the bright, beautiful green of a fragrant meadow surrounded by forest. Huckleberry, blackberry, and blueberry shrubs gave way to apple and plum trees, backed by the lofty trees of an old forest.

It sort of reminded Katie of Dad's attempt at a forest garden, although his trees weren't so old and huge. She stepped around a ring of mushrooms remembering how proud Dad was of the mushrooms he cultivated. Dad said that forest gardens required much less work and provided a diverse habitat for animals, birds, bees and microbes in the soil, as well as being more resilient in extreme weather events. He was always going on and on about it while Mom frowned and pointed at the stack of bills.

A groan startled her out of her memories. Za's wide shoulders stuck fast between the rock and the cave wall. "Help!" he yelled, straining so hard that his violet skin turned a deep plum.

"You have only to flow with the rock," said Dania. "Adapt yourself to its boundaries and let the energy work for you."

"I can't!" screamed Za. "Can't you see? I'm stuck."

The lion arched her back and roared.

Katie froze.

Dania scratched the lion behind her ears and murmured soft words.

"Keep that beast away from me!" shrieked Za.

Katie repressed a smile. Mr. Know-it-All wasn't quite as perfect as he liked to pretend.

"Hush," said Dania. "You're upsetting Kira. She's very sensitive." She placed one hand on Za's head and the other against his shoulder. With a popping sound, Za burst free.

He rubbed his shoulder, giving the lion a wary look. Kira stared back at him with implacable topaz eyes. Without taking his eyes off of the lion, Za addressed Dania, "I need your help. You see, I got lost between."

"We," corrected Katie.

"That's why I came," replied Dania, "although I do wonder at your being here. Not many stumble into the land of the Winged Ones in these times…"

Za's yellow eyes gleamed. "Can you return me to my world?"

"Only the Winged Ones can do that," replied Dania, gesturing for them to follow, "but I can shelter you for a while." She began to walk away, lithe and light, leafy patterns dappling her skin in shades of amber, brown and gold.

Katie scanned the rocky slope. The cave was so embedded in the hillside that it was nearly impossible to detect. She'd never be able to find it again. And, certainly, the way home must be near here, where she'd entered this world. Mom and Dad must be crazy worried about her by now. They might even think she'd run away after the big fight. If only she hadn't said such horrible words to them. Words she could never take back. She couldn't get the stricken expression on Mom's face out of her head.

Za shoved ahead of her and he disappeared behind a tree. Dania's words echoed in her mind: "Your only hope lies somewhere else."

"Wait!" Katie raced after them.

Sounds filled the forest. Birds called to one another in the trees, small animals rustled in the bushes. It felt different here, in this ancient forest. There was a deep hush, and her nerves relaxed a bit. Somehow she felt sheltered beneath the big trees. Their thoughts seemed slow and creaky and her own thoughts slowed down, as if she were in some sort of trance, as she walked between waist high ferns in a dreamy state. An animal that looked like a cross between a monkey and a squirrel swung from branch to branch, aiming a nut at the lion. The monkey-squirrel gibbered happily when it hit.

The lion growled.

"Never mind," soothed Dania, petting lustrous fur. "He's just a tease."

The tawny beast relaxed under her hand. Katie had never seen anyone with a pet lion. Once, at the circus, she'd watched a lion tamer who had been able to get the animals to do his bidding, but he had used a whip. This lion was as docile, at least with Dania, as Sasha was with her. God, she missed her cat.

Dania led the way briskly within the thickening forest. Trees grew so dense that they filtered the gray light of the misty day. Moist, earthy scents rose as she stepped on the mulchy forest floor. Katie shivered, forcing her tired body to keep up.

Her legs were rubbery by the time Dania stopped. "Welcome to my home."

"Excuse me," said Katie, "Do you have a bathroom?"

Dania motioned towards the creek. "I bathe in the pools."

Katie said more softly so Za wouldn't hear, "I need to pee."

"Oh, yes, I forgot," said Dania, pointing to a thick stand of huckleberry bushes. "You can go behind those."

Katie hid as well as she could. When she was done, she wiped off with a few leaves and then walked nonchalantly out from behind the hedge and looked around. She expected to see a house of some sort. Instead, in the center of thick trees, boughs converged in an arc that formed a domed shelter. "This is my living temple," said Dania, moving a branch aside to create an opening.

Once inside, Dania lit candles and put them on a flat rock. The candles reminded Katie of Mom's altar at home, where she placed flowers and shell mandalas, statues of Quan Yin and Mother Mary beneath a hanging Green Tara Thanka. There were also the two small baskets they had woven out of reeds last summer when Mom was teaching at art and music camp and they both got to go. Inside one basket, Mom had put items to represent the ancient Celtic religions of her ancestors. There was an acorn from an oak, symbol of strength, endurance, and protection. She placed a crystal shaped like a drop of water to represent water. There was a scroll with the ancient Ogham alphabet written onto it. Ogham was an entire language based on trees! A smooth brown stone was for earth, an ancient Celtic gold coin that mom said had been passed down in her family for good luck, and a fan of feathers for air. Katie's basket was still empty and Mom said that was fine as space was an important element, too. Staring at the candle Dania had lit, Katie prayed, "Por favor, please help me get home."

Dania squatted next to her and said, "I'm sure the Goddess who hears all will not forget you."

Za thrust his barrel chest out. "What about me?"

A hint of laughter twitched the corner of Dania's mouth. "You are exactly where you need to be."

"That's easy for you to say," protested Katie. "You're home." Her eyes stung with tears she refused to shed. "I may never see my parents or Sasha or my friend, Amy, again."

"True," agreed Dania, "Each day is a gift. We never know how long we have. All of us. We come and we go. We arise and we grow and hopefully bloom fully before we fade and return to the Mother again, part of the endless cycle of..."

Dania's words swam around in Katie's brain making her feel ill. The forest woman was agreeing! Katie might never see her parents again. "This is NOT helping!" Katie couldn't stop herself from interrupting.

Dania gave Katie a look full of kindness and understanding. "Things may yet work out for the best."

"Perhaps they will, if you can help me contact my guardian," said Za.

Dania nodded, her dark eyes serious. "I will certainly try. But first we must eat and rest."

CHAPTER FIVE

The Unexpected Assignment

Katie could hear Kira padding around outside. Za darted a nervous glance at the entryway. "The lion won't come in here, will she?"

"Don't worry about Kira," said Dania, rummaging around in bags of stores full of fruits, vegetables and nuts.

Katie noticed that Za still looked tense. His posture was rigid and he stared warily at the opening in the branches. She didn't feel too afraid herself. *Not with Dania around.* "Did you say food?" asked Katie, wondering how long it had been since she'd eaten. Her stomach quit growling hours ago, and now it tied itself in knots. Probably trying to eat itself.

Dania smiled. She moved with the same controlled grace as the lion as she scooped food into three hollowed pieces of wood and placed them on a large stump. It smelled delicious. Katie sat down, her mouth watering.

Za grinned. "I'm so hungry, I could eat an ontopod."

"What's an ontopod?" asked Katie.

"A large insect," replied Za between slurps. "We don't have

many animals on our worlds, so sometimes we eat insects." He made a face. "Ontopods taste the worst."

Katie, whose family was mostly vegetarian and never ate any animals other than fish, changed the subject. "This is delicious," she said, taking a bite of the creamy mash that was almost, but not quite, potatoes. "What is it?"

"I make it from forest roots," replied Dania. "Of course, I don't need to eat. The light and water are enough for me, but every once in a while, I enjoy a meal."

Katie raised her eyebrows, but she didn't bother to ask why Dania didn't need to eat. What was one more mystery when nothing made sense?

They ate in silence for a few minutes. Dania's brow furrowed in a puzzled expression. Finally she broke the silence. "Not even I can tell what is in the mind of the Goddess," she mused, "but it is possible that she sent the two of you to bring peace to the land of the Winged Ones."

Za frowned. "We weren't sent and we're not together."

Katie shot him a dirty look. Good thing she'd met Dania and he wasn't the only one she had to rely on.

Dania's fingers wove together in a steeple. "You are together."

"Pure coincidence," said Za.

"Nothing happens by accident," said Dania. "All is part of the pattern, though the pattern constantly shifts and reforms, always seeking balance, seeking beauty, playing with facets of color, light, air, vibrations, frequencies and sound. It's very complex, and impossible for even the wisest to comprehend. That's why it's so dangerous to interfere with even the smallest particle, the most delicate strand of morphing reality. Everything, everyone, affects everyone else and..."

Dania sounded like Dad. He was always rambling on about how one part of the ecosystem connected to another in a living whole. "What did you mean when you said maybe we were sent to bring peace?" asked Katie, looking around. "It's certainly peaceful here."

"The forest is peaceful," agreed Dania. "This whole world used to be an oasis of peace. But lately there has been a disturbance beyond the forest. It seems to be growing."

A chill crept over Katie. "What sort of disturbance?"

"I'm not sure. It is hard for me to see that which exists outside my forest. Perhaps if I dream..." Dania placed the wooden bowls in a stone hollow filled with water, and then she gestured to the fragrant boughs heaped against the living branch walls. "You may sleep there."

Suddenly Katie realized how tired she felt. She barely managed to crawl onto her bed of fronds and cover herself with a blanket of feathers before she plummeted into sleep.

Dreaming, big trees whispered to her, showing her a field of subtle light radiating out from the forest for a mile. Somehow in her dream it made perfect sense to Katie that the trees talked to each other within this field. "Breathe the stars," whispered an ancient oak. "Breathe the stars."

KATIE AWOKE TO SUNSHINE SPLASHING THROUGH THE leafy arch, making her blanket shine. Her eyes darted around, looking for Dania or Za. Not seeing them, Katie got up and walked towards the opening without bothering to put her shoes on.

The lion lay in front of it, lazily licking her paws. She looked so soft with her lush fur that Katie was tempted to pet her but instead circled carefully around. Even though Kira seemed gentle, she *was* a lion—and a rather large one at that.

Katie felt the squish of moss between her toes as she followed the sound of Dania's lilting voice down a path that led to a steaming pool. Dania and Za sat immersed to their necks.

"A hot spring!" exclaimed Katie, who'd never been to one before.

"This is my sacred pool," Dania announced grandly. "Come in."

Katie touched the water cautiously with the tip of her toe. It was wonderfully warm but there was no way she was taking off her clothes in front of Za. Still, she remembered she was wearing black underwear and they looked like swimsuit bottoms. Her white T-shirt needed a wash anyway, so Katie left it on, peeled off her pants, and slipped gratefully into the water. "Mmm…" Katie leaned against a smooth boulder and looked up at green leaves glistening in the morning light. Birds hopped from branch to branch, singing their greetings to the new day.

Then the air filled with static. The hairs on Katie's head spiked out like the fur on a frightened cat. Something smelled like a fresh wind blowing over ice and the space in front of Katie rippled. She edged closer to Dania. "What's going on?"

"I nee-ee-d help getting throoo…" rumbled a voice.

Za sat up fast, splashing water in Katie's face. "It's my guardian!"

Katie's heart leaped. Za's guardian would take them home!

Dania's forehead wrinkled. "Concentrate," she called to the indistinct form. "Link with me, and Kira and I will help you."

Katie stared hard, watching the haze become a cloud slowly taking shape and forming itself into an enormous being. He was all platinum light: clear sparkling hair, shiny robe with a glistening cane, and eyes that made Katie tremble. They were the color of starlight and as round as marbles.

"Thank the suns you're here!" exclaimed Za. "I was beginning to worry I'd be stuck forever." He grinned. "Now you can take me home to Stella."

"And me—to Earth," added Katie hopefully.

The guardian looked at Za and Katie with his peculiar eyes. Without a pupil, they looked sightless. "I have watched you from the beginning…"

"Then what took you so long?" asked Za, tossing his head of curly blue hair. "You must have heard me calling."

The guardian chuckled and his airy form expanded so that Katie looked right through him at the trees. "Hard not to, with you jamming the space-waves with nonstop emergency thoughts. But, there isn't much I can do."

"Not much you can do?" echoed Za, thrusting out his square chin. "What are you talking about? You're my guardian—avatar of ten galaxies, remember? Of course, you can take me home!"

The guardian waved his cane. "I don't have much authority on this world. It is not *in* the ten galaxies and, even if it were, I still would not help you. This is your journey quest."

"B-but…" spluttered Za.

The guardian continued speaking in an impassive tone. "Your initiation begins with this quest. I've started you off in the Cave of Forgetting because the only way for you to find your way home is to remember."

"Remember what?" asked Za, resting his huge purple feet against a smooth granite boulder on the edge of the pool.

"Remember yourself. Remember who you are." The guardian glanced pointedly at Za's feet. "And most important of all, remember your feet!"

Katie rolled her eyes. *How could Za ever forget those big feet?*

The guardian continued, "Naturally, you'll have to do this on your own, except for your good luck in having this Earth girl as a companion."

"No," said Katie. "Za promised you'd take us home. He said everything would be solved if we found you."

The guardian turned his starry eyes towards Katie. He stared long, as if he were measuring her. Cold swept Katie's body, and then electric heat. "You'll do, Earth child, you'll do."

Katie's face flushed. "I will not! I don't want to go on Za's quest. I want to go home!"

"Sometimes we have to do what we must, and not what we wish," the guardian replied firmly, and then turned towards Za.

Za sat stunned, opening and closing his mouth like a fish. Only a miserable croak came out. "We must hurry," said the guardian. "I haven't the energy to stay here long and before I fade, I want to give you each a gift. For you, Earth girl, I have this charm. Hold onto it, for it will help you on your journey."

Immediately Katie felt a tingling sensation on her wrist. Looking down, she saw a charm bracelet. Katie mumbled, "Thank you," but wondered, what good a silly bracelet would do. Especially since there was no way she was going on a quest with Za. *Dania will help me get home. She has to.*

"For you, Za, I have a journey song. Your journey song will harmonize you with the particular song weave of this world so that you can find your way," said the guardian, beginning to sing.

Three moons glow
On golden hills
Lake below
With songs and trills
Brings deep dreams
On petal beds
So it seems
Wake sleepy heads
Together seen
Winged Ones are
Flying serene
Home, home star

The guardian's song reminded Katie of Mom's recent composition. The words were different, but both songs had a similar tune and rhythm to Twinkle, Twinkle Little Star. As he sang, Za's guardian grew increasingly sheer until he vanished along with the last notes.

"Wait!" wailed Za, finding his voice at last. "This can't be my journey quest. No one told me. I'm not prepared. I don't even have a journey kit!"

The voice of the guardian drifted back. "You have only until the waning of the third moon to complete your quest."

CHAPTER SIX

An Unwanted Gift

Za slapped his forehead. "Guardians do this sometimes," he groaned. "There's a saying on Stella about journey quests: You never know where, you never know when. And they always involve a service that's really needed. Our worlds believe no one is truly a full adult until they've discovered how to serve. But we have no idea what the service is, and I didn't think my quest would happen like this."

"What sort of services have your people done in the past?" asked Katie.

Za stood up and stepped out of the pool. "Usually people return with a simple service like a better way to heal wounds or reduce stress, but my big sister was gifted with a seeing stone by the people of the crystal planet. The elder women of Asha use it all the time to find true knowing and guide the kinfolk." Za hopped from rock to rock, landing securely on his big feet. "Paz, an older classmate of mine, is teaching everyone on Stella the art of attention. He learned that every living being loves attention, and even some beings we don't usually consider living, like the rocks. You should see the way the plants grow when Paz is near!"

Katie didn't say anything. You didn't have to go on a quest to another world to figure that one out. Dad always talked to his plants and Mom accompanied his words with her flute. Both her parents insisted the plants grew better for the attention.

"Come," said Dania. She rose and led the way back to her leafy bower, going inside and returning with a basket of bizarre-looking fruit. Dania passed it around and Katie took what looked like a silver banana. Za picked out something round and red.

"I will aid you as I can," said Dania, settling down beside Kira and leaning her head against the lion's belly. "I sense your quest is important and may have consequences for my world and many others. All worlds are related. There are infinite connections going out beyond the beyond into the universe. Usually the songs of all creation harmonize in a symphony of beauty, but lately there are reverberations from a sour note. Perhaps that is why the Earth child was sent."

Words burst from Katie's mouth. "Why send me? I'm not some special Earth child. How could I be? It's not even my initiation." Katie paused to catch her breath and added, "I'm not going! Why should I?" Then she gave Dania a pleading look and continued more softly, "Can I please stay here with you?"

Za stopped chewing and straightened his shoulders. "I don't mind going alone," he said. "Most people go on their quests alone, although everyone's quest has different circumstances, depending upon what it is they need to learn. Anyway, who needs a stupid Earth girl?"

Katie stomped her foot on the bark and duff of the forest floor. "I'm not stupid!" Even as Katie defended herself, a small doubt nagged at her. Her grades hadn't been too good lately. But that had to be from all the troubles at home and not because she was stupid, didn't it?

A low threatening sound rumbled in Kira's throat. "Please keep your voice down," Dania said. "Shrill tones upset Kira."

Katie hung her head, wishing she hadn't lost her temper. What did she care if Za thought she was stupid? He was just a weird alien. Katie looked back at Dania, now scratching Kira's stomach so that the lion rolled on her back, exposing more of her belly, and purred—just like Sasha.

"Please let me stay here with you," she begged.

Dania's nose twitched, the way Sasha's did when she smelled something she didn't like. "It is your choice," she said, at last, "I won't stop you, but I must warn you, if you stay here you will never get home."

Katie gave Dania a hopeless look. "My only chance is to go with *him*?" she asked, staring at Za with dismay.

"Your best chance," agreed Dania. "And Za's best chance. I sense that it's possible for the two of you to succeed if you stay together. Besides, Za will need your special talent and the gift his guardian gave to you."

"What special talent?"

Before Dania had a chance to reply, Za interrupted, "I don't see what good a silly bracelet will be, even if it was from my guardian."

"I wouldn't talk," said Katie. "Your journey song doesn't even make sense." She sang a few bars:

Three moons
On a lake
Below songs

Za laughed, spraying green seeds from the bright red fruit all over Katie. "That's not how it goes."

Katie wiped off the seeds, disgusted. "It is. I never forget a tune."

"Well, you forgot this one," said Za. "Listen," he commanded, opening his mouth and singing the tune.

Katie fingered the silver banana without peeling it. How could she have forgotten such a simple song? "Let me try again."

Za shrugged. "Go ahead."

Brings deep dreams
On beds of petals
Beneath a lake

Katie stopped. This time even she could hear that she had it wrong. "Why can't I remember it?"

Za flashed his blue teeth in a grin. "That's the nature of journey songs. They're nearly impossible for anyone but the person to whom they're given to remember."

Dania arched her back against Kira in a cat-like stretch. "That's one reason you'd do best to go with Za. His journey song may guide both of you to the Winged Ones. They are the only creatures capable of taking you home."

Katie peeled the silver banana, biting into the crunchy white interior. She swallowed. "Will you come with us?"

Dania kissed Kira's nose, then stood, brushing fur off her green-gold gown. "Help me pack. If we leave now, I can guide you."

Katie ducked under a branch and followed Dania into her living temple. Noon sun shafted through gaps in the canopy, making the feather blankets glint red, green, blue. Dania stuffed two woven bark packs with fruit, flatbread and nuts. Then she folded the blankets neatly on top and tied the packs closed.

"What will we drink?" asked Katie.

"I have packed wooden cups which you can fill from the many creeks and springs."

"Is that safe?"

"Of course," answered Dania. Then she frowned. "Or it used to be. There may be places in the marsh where the water is bad. The Poison One…"

Katie stared at Dania. "What Poison One?" She shivered as she spoke the name.

Dania looked at Katie with her dark, amber flecked eyes. "From what the birds have told me, there is a Poison One fouling the waters.

"Is it a large animal?" Za asked, scratching his head. "Will it hurt us?"

"I don't know," replied Dania.

But Katie felt a strange sense of familiarity. A shadow lurked in the back of her mind and she could almost hear it murmuring. She picked up her pack. "There has to be another, safer way to go!"

"The only way to reach the golden hills is to cross the wetlands," said Dania, coming out of her tree hut and clicking her fingers to Kira. She walked briskly down the path.

Katie followed unhappily behind, noticing that Dania's light footsteps disturbed nothing and left no marks. The forest was full of sounds. Monkey-squirrels chattered overhead, birds sang, small animals scurried up and down the branches of enormous trees. Kira pounced, missing one of them by inches.

A yellow bird descended and hovered in the air before Dania, chirping to her as she walked. Dania whistled, and the bird chirped again.

Katie scrambled over a root. "Can you talk to the birds?"

"Of course," replied Dania. "I can communicate with anyone in this forest."

"I wondered why you spoke English," said Katie, hurrying to keep up.

Dania chuckled. "Is that what you think we are speaking?"

Katie nodded, shifting the pack on her back to a more comfortable position. "It's the only language I know besides the Spanish Dad's teaching me."

Dania smoothed her green-gold dress, making it shimmer like leaves in a breeze. "Well, I'm not speaking English."

"Sure sounds like English."

"Putting what I say into a language known to you is a trick of your mind. Actually we are speaking the ancient forest tongue—one nearly every creature understands, whether they know it or not. Understanding is imprinted deep in the DNA of living creatures. You know your human DNA is very similar to that of the trees?"

Katie frowned, trying to figure out what Dania meant. She knew about DNA and the double helix, but didn't understand how it could possibly help people speak some forest language. By the time she opened her mouth to ask, Dania and Za were far ahead. Za might be short but he covered a lot of ground fast with those enormous feet. Katie trotted to catch up, jumping over a fallen branch, wishing the straps on her pack didn't dig into her shoulders. The fresh fruit Dania had packed sure weighed a ton. They'd been walking for at least two hours. Za didn't even look tired. He could probably walk all day. Katie pursed her mouth and forced herself to go on. She would *not* be the first one to complain.

The forest opened up into a meadow with a fresh bubbling spring. Dania, Kira and Za waited for Katie beside a wooden footbridge. "This is as far as I can go," said Dania.

Katie looked across the bridge. There were only a few trees on the other side, and the meadow soon gave way to marsh.

"You should come with us," insisted Za. "You said yourself that my quest might be important to your world."

Dania shimmered in the afternoon sun. "Alas, it is impossible for me to go further."

"Why not?" asked Katie, continuing without waiting for an answer. "We need your help. Please, please come with us."

"I'm sorry," replied Dania. "My being is only here, in this forest." She knelt down and filled a wooden cup with the crystalline water from the spring. "Drink," she said, offering the cup to Katie. "Drink the intelligence, essence and knowing of this pure holy water."

Katie savored a sip. Sweet and fresh. A light, fizzy feeling flowed within her body.

Dania passed the cup to Za. "This water will inform you."

That didn't make sense, and yet in a way it did. It felt like the water sang in her belly, telling her how to be clear and clean, how to be well.

After Za slurped down some of the water and handed the cup back to Dania, she knelt down and gazed for a long time into Kira's eyes. Katie could see some sort of intelligence streaming between them. "I have another gift for you," said Dania. "Kira has agreed to accompany you on your journey to the golden hills."

Za groaned. "Not the lion!"

Dania smiled serenely. "I insist. That way, I may be able to follow your doings, at least in visions, and Kira will give you some protection."

"But without you," Za asked, "how do we know that lion will be tame? What if she gets hungry?"

Za had a point. Katie remembered how Kira had tried to pounce on that animal. But there was something so lovely about Dania that she couldn't help trusting her.

Dania caressed Kira's luxurious fur once, and then the lion bounded off. Katie reached for Dania. Her hand slipped through warm light and the forest lady faded before her eyes.

CHAPTER SEVEN

A Desperate Plan

Katie gaped at the place where Dania had stood. "Where did she go?"

Za shrugged. "Don't worry about that. I don't have forever. Let's go."

"Come back, Dania," cried Katie. "Oh, please come back."

The trees at the edge of the forest stood in deep green silence. The footbridge creaked as Za crossed. Katie turned in time to see Kira's tail flash in the distance far ahead of Za. "What if we can't keep up with Kira?" called Katie. "Are you sure you know the way?"

Za shouted over his shoulder, "We don't need Kira. I've got the journey song."

"That song didn't say much."

"Said enough," answered Za, pointing. "We just have to reach those golden hills."

Katie squinted. A golden haze hovered in the far distance. "How do you know those are hills and not clouds or something?"

"Easy, silly. Anyone can see..." Za stopped. "Sorry, I forgot. You are practically blind." He started walking. "Follow me."

Katie glared. To think she had no choice but to travel with this alien. But, she couldn't stay here alone. She'd never get home. And she had to get home, had to at least talk to her parents about what had happened.

She crossed the bridge and stepped onto the meadow, humming softly, trying to comfort herself with Mom's new tune. It sounded almost like a lullaby and soothed Katie's frazzled nerves.

"Can you stop making that sound?" demanded Za. "It's getting on my nerves."

"You're the one who is getting on my nerves," Katie retorted, but she quit singing. Za had ruined even that small comfort, so she walked in silence as the lush green gave way to wetlands. Frogs, dragonflies, hummingbirds, small pink butterflies and leaping fish hopped and flew and swam in the life-giving environment. A few graceful willow trees grew beside a series of ponds. The water was clear enough to see the sandy bottom with little pollywogs swimming along the grassy reeds on the edges. She jumped between stalks and stems, landing upon tufts of grass poking up from spongy soil.

Za broke the silence. "I hope that dratted lion doesn't sneak around and stalk us from behind."

"Kira is our friend," said Katie, hoping she was right. "Dania wouldn't have sent her otherwise."

"Maybe," he said, but he didn't sound like he believed it.

Sloshing in the mud, Katie lifted one foot after another. They'd been walking for hours in the beautiful watery land when suddenly Katie realized it was too quiet. Where had all the birds gone? Wetlands teemed with life. On their last family camping trip to the coastal marshes and lagoons, Katie had seen red hawks circling above, blue herons, white egrets, nighthawks, ducks, geese, and so many songbirds she'd never be able to name them all. Her favorites were the bright yellow tanagers and the small brown wrens with their melodious songs. Mom said the birds inspired her musical compositions and it was true their chirping and warbling had sounded like a symphony.

Here not even a mosquito zzzzz'd and she didn't see anything alive. *Even on this world, there should be life in a marsh.* The air filled with a musty, moldy rotting smell and the water became murky with an oily slick on top. There weren't even many plants. On their camping trip, Mom had helped her gather blackberries, dandelions, and dock. Mom was excited when they found a stand of wild nettles because she said making them into tea would be just the thing for their spring allergies. Later they gathered bull rushes to weave into future baskets. *They'd probably never do that now.* Katie's thoughts were as glum as the bleak environment as she trudged on and on.

Her knees ached by the time the sun sank lower on the horizon. *Wasn't Za ever going to stop*? "I'm starved and I have to rest."

Za plopped beside her on the small grassy island. His purple toes poked out of a coat of hardened gray mud. Throwing nuts into the air and catching them with his long tongue, like a lizard eating flies, Za turned to her and said, "We've made it this far."

Katie looked away as he flung his tongue out and curled it around a falling nut. She pulled a piece of flatbread out of her pack and took a bite. "Even if I do make it home, nothing will be the same," Katie murmured, half to herself. "For one thing, I'll never convince my parents to let me have a horse now, and that's the least of it."

"What's a horse?"

Katie tried her best to explain.

"I can't imagine why you'd want one of those monsters," said Za. "Still, your parents should get you what you want after completing a journey quest. When I get home, I'll be able to pick out my own viewer, a new orb, booster boots, and load stars and..."

"I get the point," interrupted Katie, shivering in the rising mist. "You're just as spoiled as you act."

"I am not! Everyone gets life gear when they finish their initiation. Your parents should *want* to get you a growing gift."

Katie put her head in her hands. "I'm sure they do, but..."

A spray of water cascaded over Katie as something large leapt out of the murk and belly-flopped back down. "What was that?"

"Let's get out of here!" said Za.

Katie stood on her sore knees. "Lead on."

Za turned around and around again. "Do you remember which direction we came from?"

"You're kidding, aren't you?" asked Katie, chilled by the cold fog. "Your journey song tells you the way, right?"

"Not in this fog," replied Za. "It's blocking my view of the hills."

"Great," Katie said sarcastically.

From somewhere close by, Kira growled. Za jumped into the air and came down hard on the muddy slope and his feet slid into the water. "Aagh!"

The water rippled. A humped shape headed straight for Za. It was the size of a small spinner dolphin with a bright orange body striped with fluorescent green. "Look out!" yelled Katie, watching horrified as the thing wrapped it's long toothy snout around Za's leg and pulled him down until the putrid water reached his neck.

"Help!" screamed Za, waving his hand frantically at Katie.

Katie knelt in the muck, struggling to keep a grip on Za's slimy hand. Water bubbled as his head went under.

Bending over close and holding tight, Katie yanked with all her might. The thing was too strong! She tumbled forward, her face falling towards the muddy water.

Something tugged her leather belt, dragging her and then Za, still fiercely clutching her hand so that her shoulder felt like it was being pulled out of its socket, back up the slope. Katie's shirt rode up and she felt soft fur and warm breath against her back. Kira! Katie was awed at the gentle way the lion gripped her waistband without biting.

A burbling sound susurrated up from the quagmire and the orange thing slithered back underneath, showing its smooth body one more time before disappearing in the muddy water.

Za laid against the damp slope and retched and retched. Up close, now that the water had washed away the mud, Katie noticed the bottoms of Za's feet were as thick and probably as tough as the soles of her tennis shoes. Za shuddered. "Disgusting." He rubbed the red bite marks that circled his ankle.

"Can you walk?" asked Katie.

"I'll have to. We can't stay here."

Kira stood a few paces away from Katie, looking at her intently. Then she padded away, stopped and turned.

"I think Kira wants us to follow her," said Katie.

"No way," answered Za. "If it wasn't for that lion, I wouldn't have fallen into the water in the first place, and that thing wouldn't have almost gotten me."

"Listen," said Katie, exasperated. "Kira is the only reason you didn't drown. She pulled us back up."

Za's yellow eyes grew round and wide. "I still don't think we should follow a lion. She won't know the way."

"Think what you like," said Katie, putting her pack on, "but I'm following Kira. You're lost."

Filmy fingers of fog rose from the marsh. Za stood, sweeping the goop off his brown jumpsuit. It came off easily and then the jumpsuit looked as fresh and unwrinkled as ever.

Kira bounded to the next chunk of dry grass without splashing a drop on her luxurious fur, and turned once again to stare at them. Katie followed without another word.

"That lion is probably just looking for a spot to eat us," groused Za, but he hurried after them.

Kira moved so quickly that it took all of Katie's energy to keep up. Her tennis shoes squeaked at every step and she stumbled with exhaustion. "I hope Kira stops soon," she said. "It's almost dark."

"We'll have to find a dry place to sleep," said Za.

"Yeah, right," said Katie, looking around at the dirty water that surrounded them. Her pulse slowed, as if the blood in her own body was becoming sluggish. But then she felt the sparkling fizz of the holy spring water singing in her veins, a bubbly sweet effervescence that made her feel better. "I'm thirsty too," she added, wishing she had more of that spring water, "but we obviously can't drink *this*."

At last, Katie dragged herself onto a mound of semi-dry earth. "This is as far as I can go."

Za huddled beside her, wrapping his feather blanket around his shoulders. Kira emerged out of the twilight mist and nudged Katie's knee with her nose. Katie shook her head. "I can't make it another step."

The lion seemed to understand. She lay down and put her head on her paws, watching them with one golden eye.

Katie wrapped up in the welcome warmth of her own blanket and watched the sun set. Minutes later the white searchlight of the moon peeped over the horizon, reflecting twinkles on the water. A second moon followed the first, and then a third rose and its light turned the surroundings silver. "There really are three moons."

"Of course," answered Za. "Journey songs are never wrong." He yawned. "I've got to get some sleep."

"Shouldn't one of us keep watch?"

"Sure. Wake me when it's my turn."

Great. Za never thought about anybody but himself. He hadn't even thanked her for helping pull him out of the water, and now he didn't ask if she *could* stay awake. She tried to keep her eyes open, shifting uncomfortably on the prickly grass. Impossible to get comfortable. Kira stretched besides her, warm and cozy, purring. Like Sasha, thought Katie, unable to resist leaning against the lion's soft belly. Moons swam blearily before her tired eyes. *Cats like to stay awake at night*, Katie told herself, letting them shut just for a minute. She forced them open again in spite of the burning, then told herself, *Kira will protect us*, and let them close once and for all.

THE LOW RUMBLE IN KIRA'S THROAT STARTLED KATIE awake. Wind from heavy wings batted against her face. Something large hovered above them. "What?!"

Za didn't have a chance to answer before it swooped down and seized the two of them in its claws.

Kira's roar howled after them on the wind.

CHAPTER EIGHT

It's Hungry!

Katie's arm pinched where the monster gripped her. The nails on its claws curved over her shoulder and down her chest. "Kira!" she screamed, clutching her feather blanket, trying not to look down.

The beast snorted sulfurous clouds that looked yellow in the moonlight. It screeched a deafening sound, like the cry of hundreds of wailing babies. Suddenly it lost altitude and Katie's stomach gave a sickening lurch. "Don't let me die," she prayed. "Please don't let me die without seeing Mom and Dad and Sasha again."

Sharp talons released their hold on Katie's shoulder and she thudded onto solid ground.

"Katie!" yelled Za. "Are you there?"

"Run!" she hollered, forcing her wobbly legs to move.

A firecracker boom thundered and the air filled with a nauseating smell. Even breathing through her mouth, the odor came so thick it coated Katie's tongue with a foul taste. *Hard to run. Hard to breathe. Have to keep going. Only hope. Have…to…keep…going.*

The monster extended a scaly forearm, plucked them from the ground, and set them right in front of its mouth. "STAY."

"You sp-sp-speak English?" asked Katie.

"Of course I speak English!" answered Za. "What's wrong with you?"

"Not you," said Katie, pointing. "Didn't you hear it say STAY?"

"You're imagining things," said Za, grabbing her arm. "Let's go before it kills us."

Katie pulled her arm away. "Running is no use. Look how easily it caught us."

"ME NEED HELP!" roared the beast.

Katie gathered all her courage and looked straight up to where the monster's small head perched atop its massive body. "Why do you need help?"

"NO FEEL WELL."

"How come?" asked Katie. If she could keep it talking, maybe they'd have a chance to escape.

The monster patted its midsection with a claw. "HURTS."

Za nudged her. "How do you know what it is saying? All I hear from that beast is screeching."

Katie frowned, puzzled. But there was no time to figure out why only she could understand when Za was the one with the gift of tongues. She had to keep it talking. "Why does it hurt?"

"COME," said the monster, pushing her forward with a hot nose. "ME SHOW."

Za gave Katie a terrified look. "Where is it taking us?"

Katie stumbled on a loose rock. Hot air burned the back of her pants. "Slow down," she begged. "We can't walk this fast."

"ME AM GO SLOW," it replied, covering a huge distance with each stomp. "ME FLY YOU?"

"No!" cried Katie, rubbing her sore shoulder.

"What's it saying?" hissed Za.

"It offered to fly us."

"Guardian forbid!"

Katie ran as fast as she could over the boulder-strewn terrain, struggling to keep ahead of the beast's searing breath. At last, the creature stopped a few inches away from an enormous, cracked egg.

"THIS WHERE ME COME."

"This is where you hatched?" Katie touched the rim of the egg. It was still warm.

The beast thumped its tail twice, then toppled over, falling on its own foot. "EEEEE!" it cried, without moving off the foot. "HURTS. HURTS. HURTS." Hard rock tears that looked like emeralds hailed around them.

"Of course it hurts," Katie yelled, dodging the tears. "You're sitting on your foot."

It rolled off the foot, snuffled a few times, and then, much to Katie's relief, quit crying. It was nothing but a baby. Katie shoved one of the tears into her pocket. If this was an emerald and she ever made it home, maybe they could at least afford riding lessons again. "I don't think it wants to hurt us," she whispered to Za.

The animal opened its mouth and burped green steam.

When Katie could breathe again, she said, "Can't you stop that?"

"YOU HELP."

"Yes, of course," said Katie, blinking her stinging eyes. She didn't have the faintest idea how to help a baby monster with indigestion, but she had to pretend. Maybe it wouldn't hurt them if it thought she could help. "How long have you had this problem?" she asked in her best doctor voice.

"ME HATCH. NO ONE HERE. ME LONELY. ME HUNGRY. ME EAT."

This was going to be slow. It felt like talking to a two-year-old—and not a very bright one at that. But perhaps that had its advantages. Maybe she could trick it somehow and get away. "What did you eat?"

The creature crunched a boulder underfoot. "THOSE."

"What's going on?" asked Za.

"It's a baby. It has a tummy ache."

Za rolled his eyes. "If this is a baby, I'd hate to meet one of the parents."

Katie nodded. Za was right. There was no way she wanted to meet Mom. She'd have to think of something soon.

"BELLY HURTS," moaned the creature, blasting them with a puff of steam.

"Hush," said Katie, glancing nervously at the sky. She forced her voice to stay calm and soothing. "Rocks can't be right, even for you. I wonder what animals of your sort are supposed to eat."

"DO YOU KNOW WHAT ME IS?" asked the creature, bending its long neck, and placing its head low enough for Katie to look right into its whirling multi-colored eyes. "SEEN ANY LIKE ME?"

"Let me think," murmured Katie, trying to control the trembling in her voice. "You are as big as a baby whale, you fly, and you have scales, a tail and fiery breath. Yes!!! You remind me of a dragon."

The beast fluffed his wings. "CAN TELL WHAT DRAGONS EAT?"

"Of course," replied Katie, without thinking. "There are lots in my books of fairy tales, and they always eat…" She broke out into a sweat and bit her tongue just in time. *The dragons in her books liked to eat young girls!*

The dragon flapped its wings. "TELL!"

Katie looked around desperately. There had to be something for it to eat besides herself. The bleak land didn't offer much: only that thing that almost got Za in the bog. "I think your stomach would feel better if you ate the large orange things that swim in the marsh."

The dragon's eyes whirled dizzyingly. "IS VERY LARGE, MAYBE TOO BIG ME CATCH."

"No," said Katie, looking away to stop the dizzy feeling the dragon's spinning eyes gave her. "They are much smaller than you are. It'd be easy for one as big and strong as you to catch them."

"THEY YUMMY TASTE?"

"Delicious," lied Katie, who figured they must taste disgusting. "They are juicy and sweet, not like those awful rocks. The swimmers of the marshland are moist and meaty and will make your tummy feel better." Katie crossed her fingers behind her back, hoping that the dragon would believe her story.

The dragon's eyes suddenly stopped whirling and the beast beat its wings excitedly. "ME GO. EAT NOW."

Katie watched, awed at the speed with which the dragon launched its heavy bulk into the air and over the gigantic boulders.

"Whew," said Za.

Katie grasped her feather blanket. "Let's get out of here while we can. Thank goodness the fog has lifted. Which way should we go?"

"Actually, I don't know," said Za, hanging his head. "I can't see the hills from here."

CHAPTER NINE

Enemies in the Swamp

Katie groaned. “Some good that journey song does. If only we still had Kira, she’d know the way.”

“Anywhere is better than hanging around here and waiting for that monster or its mother to come back,” replied Za, heading in the opposite direction from the one the dragon had taken.

Katie scrambled after him, hoping the dragon spent a long time hunting.

Za walked briskly despite the limp he’d had ever since that orange thing bit him. “I wonder why you could understand the dragon when I couldn’t.”

“I don’t know,” replied Katie, “but I sure wish I hadn’t left my pack behind when it snatched us. I’m starved.”

“Why didn’t you sleep with it like I did?” asked Za. “Anyway, this is no time to eat. If we don’t get out of here, *we’ll* be the ones eaten.”

Katie nodded. She felt wretched. Tired. Cold. Hungry. She trotted and walked, walked and trotted over the rocky ground. It was hard to see in the dimming light of the setting moons, one of which was waning. If this moon was already waning, how long would it be before the third moon waned? "What happens if you don't finish your quest on time?"

"Don't worry about that," replied Za, laughing. "Of course I'll finish on time."

For once his arrogant attitude cheered Katie up. If Za didn't finish before the third moon waned he'd fail his initiation but then his guardian would probably come and take him home. Katie hoped he'd figure out a way to get her home as well. "Can you sing your journey song again?"

"Sure," replied Za, guarding his foot as he made his way over a boulder.

Three moons glow
On golden hills
Lake below
With songs and trills
Brings deep dreams
On petal beds
So it seems
Wake sleepy heads
Together seen
Winged Ones are
Flying serene
Home, home star

"Do you think the Winged Ones will be at the golden hills?" Katie asked hopefully.

Za nodded. "I think so."

Katie stumbled. "It's getting hard to see."

"Not with my excellent night vision."

"I wish you'd quit bragging," groused Katie, but she followed close behind, knowing that they had to get away.

Za's shoulders went stiff with haughty silence. Too proud to take the slightest criticism. Katie tried to think of something to say that wouldn't offend him. She needed to talk. She needed to distract herself from sore knees, aching back, and mostly from how much she missed her parents and Amy and Sasha. "So how come your parents live on different worlds?"

"What a question!" Za's head swiveled all the way around, so that his face stared at her from the back of his body.

The sight made Katie feel sick. "You're going to trip if you don't turn around."

Ignoring her suggestion to turn his head back around, Za explained, "Everyone in the ten galaxies knows the importance of spending most of their time on the planet of their birth. People need the soil of their home planet to root and thrive."

"People don't have roots," Katie said shortly, sick of Za's condescending attitude.

Za stopped walking. He wriggled his long knuckled toes. "Roots can be energetic, silly. They can be emotional, social, or simply the ability to receive. Even you have roots, whether you know about them or not."

The way Za was lecturing reminded her of her teacher, Mr. Pinski. Katie exhaled a long sigh.

"It's so important to be rooted where we belong," continued Za, "Otherwise folks tend to sicken."

Home. That's where I belong. Katie gazed disgustedly at the endless field of boulders. They were all sizes. Some smooth and golden, some brownish red, or streaked with serpentine green. Definitely nothing like the rolling green hills of home with her small town nestled comfortably between.

"I mostly live on Stella because that's where I was born," Za continued, "but I often visit my mother on Asha. When my father can get time off of his work designing self-cleaning wrinkle-free jumpsuits," Za continued, gesturing proudly to his brown suit, "then he comes with me. And Mom visits us on Stella every chance she gets."

"Sounds complicated," said Katie, thinking her own life was going to be a lot more complicated when she had to live in two houses. If she ever made it home.

Za waved his hand airily. "We Stellans can handle a little complication, no problem…" Za's backward-facing head grinned at Katie, while his forward-facing body walked straight into a deep puddle.

"Serves you right," muttered Katie but she gave him a hand out of the water.

And then Za said what Katie had been too busy helping him to notice. "We're back at the swamp."

"It's practically dark!" cried Katie. "We can't wade in the marsh now. We won't be able to see that orange thing coming. We have no idea how many of them live here," added Katie, surprised that anything at all survived in this swamp. It was eerie and quiet with no signs of life. *What did those orange things even eat? Marsh weeds?*

"I hate those things," said Za, "But at least we'd have a chance with them. The dragon could eat us both in one gulp." Za took a step into the sludge. "We have to get as far away from it as possible."

"Not at night," said Katie, standing her ground. "Not without Kira. Not when I can't see."

"I can see fine," replied Za, continuing to walk, squishing mud between his long crooked toes. "Just follow me."

"Kira!" screamed Katie, desperate.

No answer. Just the soft hiss of the marsh breeze rustling the grass.

And then Katie realized why she shouldn't have screamed. They were back at the swamp! The dragon could be nearby, and if it heard her scream... Katie broke into a sweat, remembering the way she'd tricked it. What if eating the big marsh creatures had given it even worse indigestion? Would the dragon want revenge? "Where did you go?" Katie called softly.

"Over here," said Za, urging, "Come on."

"The dragon is hunting in this marsh right now," insisted Katie.

Za's breath whistled out. "I know, that's why we're trying to get away while it has something else on its mind," he said in a don't-be-a-dummy sort of voice.

"You don't understand," continued Katie. "We've got to hide until morning. It won't find us then. Dragons sleep for most of the day."

Za stopped picking his way across the mudflats. "They do? How do you know?"

"I've read about them."

"I didn't know they had dragons on your world," said Za, turning back.

Katie didn't explain that the books were fairy tales. Mom always told her that a lot of old wisdom was hidden in fairy tales, so Katie figured there was a chance the stories were right about dragon habits. Anyway, she'd feel safer traveling when she could see. Katie pointed to a large overhanging boulder. "We can hide under there until dawn."

Za squished under the narrow shelter with her, propping his foot up against the rock. "My ankle hurts."

"No wonder," Katie said. "It's really swollen."

"I wonder if that orange thing was poisonous?" asked Za, carefully inspecting his wound before rummaging in his pack.

Katie frowned. "Do you think *it* could be the Poison One?" As soon as she said the name, she felt something in the back of her mind stir.

Za frowned, but he didn't answer. He pulled out a piece of fruit.

Katie stared hungrily.

Za bit off the peel and squirted the juice onto his ankle.

"What are you doing?" demanded Katie. "We're half-starved and dying of thirst and you waste fruit!"

"I'm hoping the acid from this fruit will help heal it."

"More likely the juice will attract flies, or whatever they have on this world," Katie said grouchily. Her stomach growled. She forced herself not to say more. There was no way she was going to beg.

Za finally looked up. "Here," he said, handing her a firm green fruit. "Enjoy it, because we're going to have to ration now that you lost your pack."

Katie's face burned. Oh, why hadn't she kept her pack on, like Za? It was humiliating to be dependent on his charity. She bit hungrily into the fruit, letting the tart juice trickle down her parched throat.

After her small meal, Katie huddled in the narrow space under the boulder, curling herself into a ball for heat. She shivered, missing Kira's soft warm fur, missing Sasha, missing her own bed, missing home. At last she dozed lightly, dreaming of green rolling hills interspersed with stands of trees—firs, pines, cedars, hemlock and spruce—on knolls bordering pastureland. She dreamed of home.

Too soon the steel-gray light of dawn woke her from slumber.

Za grimaced as he stood on his swollen ankle. "Let's go."

The squelch of their feet was the only sound in the vast silence of gray sky, gray water and scraggly marsh grass. Katie hoped they weren't heading back towards Dania's forest. They'd never find the Winged Ones then, never get home. "Do you see the golden hills?"

Za hobbled on. Step, limp, step. "I caught a glimpse through the fog."

"How come you didn't tell me?"

Za shrugged. "You wouldn't have been able to see them with *your* vision." He gave her a pitying glance. "It must be hard walking around half-blind."

"You could have at least told me when you saw the hills," complained Katie.

"Well, you didn't really need to know. And those hills are huge. They look more like mountains to me. It's going to be a tough climb and I didn't want to scare you. Besides, this is my journey quest and it's up to me to make the big decisions."

"I'm on this quest too!" snapped Katie, "and I can think for myself."

"How can you do that when you've been raised on a planet like Earth?" Za asked cheerfully.

Katie kicked a dirt clod wishing it was Za. "Earth is as good as any other planet. Better! She's beautiful and blue-green and has so many different ecosystems."

"Ecosystems your species is destroying."

"Not all of us!" shouted Katie, beginning to lose her temper. "Not my dad!"

"Calm down," said Za. "We'll never get there if you keep having temper tantrums."

Hot waves of anger rolled off Katie. She wasn't having a temper tantrum! Za was just so rude and insulting. What was she supposed to do? Just put up and take all his insults, one after another?

"We're much closer," Za said conversationally. "We just have to make it over this last stretch of water."

Katie looked up. Never mind Za and his superiority complex. He was right. They had to cross the water, if you could call this nasty liquid water, and finish the quest and go home. Then she'd never have to see him again. Katie stared at the lifeless gray bog, wondering how they were going to cross it when Za could barely walk. Her flesh goose-bumped in the gummy mist. My god she hated this fog. It was nothing like the soft mists of healthy wetlands. This fog smelled rank, and was a dirty gray. She tried to hum Mom's comforting tune but her voice was thin and reedy, dampened and disappeared in the fog.

Za limped steadily in the wet and Katie lagged further and further behind him, with only her unhappy thoughts for company. *What was the use anyway? They'd never survive this quest. Besides, why trust Za? He probably made it up about the hills being closer just to sound superior.* She certainly hadn't seen any hills.

Katie stepped out of the cold gray fog into a patch of thick warm fog. "That's right, you can't trust him," said a strange, disembodied voice. "He's alien, different."

Peering past the gray shadows, Katie strained her eyes trying to see who had spoken. The voice echoed damply in the fog, muffled and indistinct, but coming from all around, both inside and outside her head. Her ears rang and a static, like when she didn't quite tune a radio station in, buzzed along with the words.

"Bring her to me!" commanded the eerie voice, and instantly leaden shapes formed in the fog, their ghostly bodies swaying and undulating all around her in a spooky dance.

"Z..." she opened her mouth to call Za, but a foggy hand clamped across it, muffling her.

The air in front of Katie became warmer and warmer until it sprayed hot steam into her face. "Come to me. I'm waiting..."

Katie felt sick. *That voice reminded her of the voice lurking in the back of her mind when Dania mentioned the Poison One. Surely, they must be related?* She tried to scream but the sound she made was barely audible. Fog fingers muted her. "Za!" she croaked.

"He won't come," the voice whispered hotly in her ear. "Instead my fog-men will bring you to me. I am their Master! Come!"

The fog-men pushed against her in a wet wave. Katie fought against them, trying to keep her feet planted firmly in the sludge, but it was so slippery. "You can't fight me," said the voice. "You are weak, small, bad. It's your fault things aren't okay at home."

How does this voice know about the troubles at home? Katie's whole body started to shake. Her knees went weak and she stumbled forward several steps. She couldn't see anything in the thick fog, but the fog-men pressed against her as if they knew exactly where they were going. "The problems at home aren't my fault," she defended herself, but her words came out in a thin whisper. Mom had looked devastated. And she'd never seen Dad like that, as if the stuffing was knocked right out of him.

CHAPTER TEN

Like a Ride?

Katie dropped to her knees, clamping her hands over her ears to block out the voice. Something sharp dug into her hip, hurting. Heat swirled around her. What was happening? Why were there pockets of hot steam in the midst of the chilly fog? And whatever it was had a voice, a horrible voice.

The heat intensified, hotter and hotter, making her arms burn. Hotter than the previous hot steam. Katie peeked up and watched as blasts of the searing heat turn the fog-men to vapor, dissipating them into scattered fragments and wisps until those too evaporated. The fog demons were gone.

Katie took her hands off her ears and cautiously sat up. A few yards away stood the dragon. Katie inhaled sharply and blurted, "Y-y-you're bigger!"

The dragon thumped its tail eagerly, sending a deluge of dank water over Katie and boasted, "Yes, indeed." It licked its lips with a long green tongue.

"You're speaking differently too," Katie noticed. *So much for her theory about the orange thing in the swamp being the Poison One; since the dragon ate it and the fog demons were still here serving their Master, that couldn't have been it.*

"Now that I've had some proper nourishment, my dragon memory cells have been activated. Why did you call?" asked the dragon.

She hadn't called! *Had the dragon heard her heart in fear calling, like Dania? That didn't seem possible; the dragon was nothing like the benevolent forest lady. Maybe fear put out radio waves or some sort of scent?* She knew many animals could sense fear. "I-I didn't call," she stammered. She'd been trying to get away from this dragon. The dragon sounded so rational and grown up now, but she still didn't trust it. Dragons in fairy tales were totally unpredictable.

"You must have something of mine," said the dragon.

Katie's mind raced. What could she possibly have that belonged to the dragon? She stood up slowly, wringing the gooey water out of her hair, rubbing the sore place on her hip. And then she remembered; her hip hurt because of the hard emerald she'd stashed in her pocket.

Katie worked her fingers into the tight opening of her damp pocket and wriggled the stone out. "Is this it?" she asked, holding the emerald up.

"Yes."

Katie's heart skipped a beat. "I'm sorry," she croaked. "I didn't think you'd mind since it was only one of your tears, and there were so many..." Her voice trailed off, and then she added, remembering from stories that dragons love to be flattered, "It was so pretty and green, like your lovely scales."

"Don't be sorry," said the dragon, twitching its green-blue tail. "I wouldn't have been able to find you if you hadn't had part of my body."

Great. Why had she been stupid enough to pick up anything belonging to a dragon? Her eyes darted around searching for Za.

The dragon continued, "After eating dozens of those delicious swimmers, my body filled with knowing ancient dragon lore. Immediately, I understood that all dragons work with the energy of the planetary bodies. There are song lines of power running throughout the cosmos and all the worlds. We dragons travel on them, each in our own way."

"Why are you telling me this?" Katie looked around the marsh trying to find Za.

"I owe you a favor for helping me figure out what to eat, and I thought understanding the enormous importance of dragons would serve you well now and in the future," the dragon said, stretching long claws and looking at its nails with almost the same expression Mom had when she was thinking about getting a manicure. "Fire dragons streak round the heavens consorting with stars, bringing light and warmth to the darkest places. Sometimes they slip into black holes and find themselves in points so dense that space and time warp and the fire dragon ends up in a stellar nursery. The dragon bursts out of this black hole nursery in jets of material that birth new stars in new galaxies."

The dragon gave Katie the same are-you-following-me look her teacher, Mr. Pinski, gave her in math. She wasn't following, but she did just what she did in class and nodded her head.

That must have satisfied the dragon because the lecture continued. "Wherever they find themselves, fire dragons stimulate nature and help quicken evolution. Water dragons rain down from the sky, filling springs, aquifers, creeks, rivers, lakes, lagoons and shining silver seas. They swim in oceans so deep they are bottomless, flowing life force everywhere."

Katie shifted from foot to foot, listening with half an ear. *Come on, Za. Where are you?*

The dragon continued droning on. "Air dragons inspire wherever they go, gusting in new ideas, blowing them on breezes of imagination, gliding across the cosmos exhaling the sweetness of creation."

Pausing, the dragon gave her an expectant look. "That's interesting," Katie said politely.

The dragon didn't take its gaze off of her. *Clearly waiting for a more enthusiastic response.* Katie asked a question to keep it talking while she watched for Za. "What kind of dragon are you?"

"I am a female earth dragon," she said, thumping her tail proudly on the ground so that the earth beneath Katie's feet trembled. "Earth dragons see, hear and sense the song weaves that crisscross in intricate webs on all the worlds. When these song weaves are damaged or torn, we earth dragons help heal and reconnect them. In the process, sometimes we rise up like volcanos, sink into the deepest craters, compress into hard rocks, and sift into the softest sand. We create new forms out of the songs. These songs can also be perceived as colors, light, sensations, knowing, and sometimes we can even smell them. But whether it is fragrance or melody, dazzling light or sweet sensation, it is all part of the song weave that we dragons help shape into all bodies, including your own."

"How do you do that?" asked Katie. *If Za didn't come back soon, maybe she should continue on to the golden hills on her own and hopefully meet him there?* She'd never find him in this marsh. And she never wanted to meet those fog-men again or hear that horrid voice.

"I take the smallest baby particle, you might call it an atom, and project the spirit from my heart inside. Then new forms arise. That's according to the lore, of course," added the dragon, twisting her neck thoughtfully. "I haven't had a chance to try it yet."

"Thank you for sharing so much with me," said Katie, continuing her polite tactic, "but I've got to find my companion now. We really have to be going. You see, we're on a quest to find the Winged Ones."

The dragon's eyes whirled thoughtfully. "I suppose I'm a Winged One myself."

Katie gulped. The dragon did have wings! But how could she trust a dragon to fly her home? It had been agony being clutched in her claws. "Can you travel between worlds?" asked Katie, half hoping the answer was 'yes' and praying equally hard that it was 'no'.

The dragon's eyes whirled faster and faster, blurring into a crazy kaleidoscope of colors. Katie looked away, too dizzy to watch. At last the dragon cleared her throat with a soft grating sound and answered, "I can't travel between planets. As an Earth dragon, I'm bound to the soil of my birth world."

Katie's shoulders sagged with relief. And then tensed with disappointment. Would she ever find the Winged Ones who would take her home?

"Besides, I found another egg like the one I hatched from." The dragon patted her belly with her short forearm, as if remembering her recent indigestion. "It would have been much easier for me if there had been an older dragon to instruct me on what to eat and drink and how to learn dragon ways." Her eyes finally stopped spinning. "I don't want to leave the new baby alone."

"No," agreed Katie, "you definitely wouldn't want to do that. You'd better go back and check on the egg. The baby could start hatching any minute."

"First could you please scratch under my chin?" she asked, laying her head down at her feet. "The new scales growing in itch and I simply cannot reach them on my own."

Katie reached her hand out and gingerly stroked its spiny throat. It felt a bit like scratching a cactus and Katie took care to scratch between the spines so that she would not get pricked.

"Mmmmm," purred the dragon.

"Katie!" yelled Za, emerging through a tall stand of pampas grass. "I've been looking everywhere. Thank the guardians..." Za froze in his tracks, his jaw hanging open.

"Za and I have to continue on our quest now," said Katie in a carefully soothing tone.

Instantly the dragon lifted her head. "I'd like to help you. Teaching you a little dragon lore certainly doesn't seem like enough to repay you for the enormous service that you did for me. Where are you headed?"

Hesitating for just a second, Katie finally replied, "To the golden hills."

"Don't tell it where we're going!" shouted Za. "Are you crazy?!"

"I can fly you there," said the dragon, ignoring Za.

"That won't work," replied Katie. "It hurts when you carry us in your claws."

"That's not a problem." The dragon gusted a small sulfurous breath. "You can climb up and ride upon my neck. It's very safe."

Katie looked around the hateful marsh. It was still a long way to the other side. She couldn't even see it yet, although the fog was gone for now. It would be back as soon as the dragon, with her hot air, left. Then they wouldn't be able to tell which way they were going. And they might meet those awful fog-men again. No, she'd rather take her chances on the dragon's back.

"What's it saying?" called Za without taking a single step closer.

"She," corrected Katie, "She says the marsh swimmers were yummy," explained Katie. "Now the dragon wants to do us a favor and fly us to the hills."

"No!" shouted Za.

"Yes!" argued Katie. "We can't keep slogging in this water, going around in circles. And besides, there's something else out here, maybe worse. Za, I heard a...a voice," stammered Katie as she recalled the wet fog fingers closing over her mouth.

"You hear things talking all the time," huffed Za. "I can get us there. We don't need a dragon."

"I know you're scared of large animals," Katie said. "But this is a *friendly* dragon."

"I'm not scared!" yelled Za, moving a few paces further away, deeper into the pampas grass. "I'd just rather trust my own feet."

"Your foot is injured and the dragon says there are plenty of those orange things. We don't want to run into them again," Katie said firmly. "Besides when the fog rises you can't see the hills and then you don't know which way to go."

The dragon lowered her body. "We should be going now. I'd like to get back to the egg. It smelled like it's about to hatch."

"Come on, Za," called Katie. "We're going."

Za turned the other way and bolted into the swamp, tripping and limping on his injured ankle.

The dragon flew over to him and reached out a scaly claw, plucking Za up by the blue hair and plunking him on her neck. "Help!" screamed Za. "Oh, great guardian, if ever you cared for me, please help me now!"

Katie winced. Being picked up by the hair must hurt. Za slipped down the dragon's long neck, flailing his arms desperately for balance.

Then the dragon laid her head at Katie's feet and Za shot the other way, sliding back towards the head. "Please climb up now," said the dragon.

Katie carefully picked her way over the scales of the dragon's chin and cheeks, settling herself onto a soft patch of skin behind the ears. The dragon lifted her head, and Katie turned to give Za a hand before he slid back down the length of the neck. "Come up behind her ears," she said. "It's actually rather comfortable here, nice and warm and there aren't any scales."

Za pulled himself up until he reached an ear then clutched it until his normally purple knuckles turned white. He gazed straight ahead without saying one word as the heavy beast lumbered into the sky.

The flight was smooth, almost like being on a super jet. Katie's hands were burning hot from the dragon's body, but she didn't dare relax her grip. It was a long way down. They sped past something sienna gold. "Kira?!" Katie yelled.

But they whooshed by so fast, Katie couldn't tell if it *was* Dania's lion. She couldn't look down anymore, anyway. Her stomach felt sick. Katie took in a few deep breaths and kept her eyes on the velvety ear she clung to, watching fascinated as the green blood pulsed through a vein in the delicate stretchy skin.

It wasn't long before the speeding dragon reached the other side of the wetlands. She landed in a clumsy bumping thumping fashion, which made Katie grateful for her secure spot behind her ear.

"Time to get off," said the dragon, lowering herself to the ground.

Katie crawled around the ear onto the slippery scales of the forehead. Za pressed against Katie in his urgency to dismount, causing her to lose her grip and tumble the rest of the way down the nose. Fortunately it was soft, just like the backs of the ears.

Za landed right beside her and immediately turned away from the dragon to stare longingly up at the golden hills, which were tall and steep and most definitely mountains and not just hills.

The dragon said, "Little purple one!"

Katie watched as the dragon picked up a clod of earth and squeezed it with her right claw. When she unfurled her long nails, the earth had become a small, hard brown pebble which she dropped on the ground beside Za. "This is for you. Remember earth!"

Za didn't even notice the pebble. He continued to face away from the dragon. "Look, Katie!" he exclaimed. "We're at the base of the golden mountains."

"The dragon's trying to tell you something, Za," said Katie.

"You know I can't understand a thing she says," replied Za. "It sounds like rumbling or growling or shrieking to me."

"Look!"

Za finally turned around. "What?"

Katie pointed at the pebble. "That."

The dragon used a claw to shift the pebble closer to Za. As soon as Za picked it up, the dragon inclined her long head towards Za and dipped her head as if she were satisfied. Then she turned to Katie and looked at her with whirling kaleidoscopic eyes. After a moment, the dragon shut one eye in what looked like an unmistakable wink, and then she launched herself into the air.

"Goodbye!" called Katie, "Gracias. Thank you." Katie held up the emerald. "I was going to give this back to you!"

The green stone blazed in the bright sun and slowly dissolved in her hand until it formed a tiny pool which splashed down onto the ground. So much for bringing an emerald home. It had looked like it was worth a lot, too. Katie wiped her hands on the grass, making the silver charm bracelet on her wrist tinkle. And then she noticed—one of the charms looked exactly like the dragon. Katie showed it to Za. "Do you think having this charm is the reason the dragon helped us over the wetlands?"

"It wouldn't be anything that simple," scoffed Za. "Besides, I could've gotten us across the swamp. No, the charm must have been for something big, like making us meet the dragon in the first place."

"Why would your guardian *want* us to meet a dragon?" asked Katie. "I know it worked out, but I was scared. Dragons are impulsive and volatile. My books say they're so capricious that you never know what they're going to do," she said, sharing more fairy tale information since that was all she had. "It might not have ended so well. I thought your guardian was on our side."

Za shrugged. "Maybe my guardian decided meeting a dragon was part of the experience I need to overcome fear. Overcoming fear is one of the steps to being initiated."

"I don't want to overcome fear," said Katie. "It's not my initiation. All I want to do is to get home."

Za snorted. "Of course it's your initiation too. Otherwise you wouldn't be here."

"Initiated into what?"

Za shrugged. "That's for you to figure out." He started limping up the slope.

Katie picked up the brown pebble. "Don't forget your gift."

"It's just an ordinary stone."

"The dragon turned plain earth into a rock! I saw her do it. She told me she's an earth dragon, and their gift is to create forms. And the dragon told *you* to remember, which is exactly what your guardian said you have to do."

Za reached out his hand for the pebble and slipped it into the hip pocket of his amazingly clean and unwrinkled jumpsuit. "You're right. Maybe it *is* important." He turned and took another step up the hill. "We'd better hike up this mountain and find the Winged Ones."

"Wait," said Katie. "If your theory is right, and the charm bracelet actually brought the dragon to us, then I think we'd better look at the rest of these charms and see who else we are going to meet."

Katie sat down in the grass at the base of the mountains and looked at her bracelet. She fingered the charm of a little fairy with wings. Was it possible to meet a fairy on this world? Sometimes she saw little lights in the mixed conifer forest Dad had planted at the back of their property on the hillside he was reforesting. And sometimes she even heard something that might be tinkling laughter. Amy always teased her and said she was imaginative. But Katie still thought maybe there were fairies in the forest, little nature spirits. She'd always wanted to actually see one. Just not on another world.

Katie glanced at the rest of the charms: a tree and an exquisite silver horse. She'd love to meet a horse. Horses always understood her, even when none of the kids at school—sometimes not even Amy—really did. Horses seemed to know how she felt. She'd volunteered to muck the stalls at the local stables to be around them and before her parents started arguing they'd even paid for lessons. But Mom said they couldn't afford her riding classes any longer.

She stroked the smooth, silver horse charm before moving on to the next one—the face of an old man with a long beard, a bit like Santa Claus, only this face was scowling. Still, how scary could a grumpy old man be? Katie stared at the last charm, wincing as she noticed the large, sharp pincers of a frightful scorpion. There was no way she wanted to meet a scorpion.

Katie brainstormed for a moment. Then it hit her. If she got rid of the charm, then maybe they wouldn't meet the scorpion. Katie tugged hard, trying to pull the scorpion charm off of her bracelet, but nothing happened. She'd have to take the whole bracelet off. Katie turned it around, looking for a clasp, but there wasn't one, and the bracelet was too tight to pull over her hand. With a sick feeling, Katie remembered the tingling sensation on her wrist when Za's guardian had made it magically appear. She kept pulling, but she knew it was no use. She'd never get *this* bracelet off.

CHAPTER ELEVEN

Things Aren't As Peaceful As They Seem

"Come on, Katie," hollered Za. "I found another spring."

Katie gave one final, futile tug at the scorpion charm before dashing a little way up the mountain to the clear bubbling water. She drank and drank, rolling the clean taste around her mouth. Then she scrubbed her face and hands with water and sand, and even rinsed her hair as best she could, the way she always did on family camping trips.

There were tracks all around the spring. This must be a favorite watering hole for all sorts of animals. Katie noticed a lion print. If only it belonged to Kira.

Some of the terror of being lost on another world washed away with the sparkling water. Katie sprawled on a huge rock slab, letting her hair dry in the sun. "I was about to die from thirst."

"Honestly, I don't know how your species has managed to survive," observed Za.

"Just because you can go two weeks without water," grumbled Katie. She lay in the soothing warmth, too tired and comfortable to complain about Za's typical conceit. Besides, it probably wasn't true about him being able to go two weeks. He'd certainly lapped up the water as fast as he could.

"My foot doesn't look right," said Za in a strained voice.

"No kidding," said Katie, staring at the green and yellow pus oozing from blistering sores. "I think it's infected. Maybe it will help if you soak it in the cold water?" Katie fought down a feeling of dread. How was Za going to hike with his foot looking like that? And what were they going to do if he couldn't hike?

Za eased his foot into the water. "It will get better. I just need to give my foot a rest."

Katie hoped so as she sprawled on a nearby rock slab, letting her hair dry in the sun for a while before she braided it again. She lay on her belly in the comforting warmth, so tired she could barely move. Her body melted into the smooth granite, shiny black mica chips embedded in the rock twinkling up at her. It was such a relief to be out of the polluted marsh. Here, there was life: buzzing bees busily seeking nectar from little blue flowers, a small brown bird singing in the bushes, the tap-tap-tap of a woodpecker. The sound of the bubbling spring lulled her, and Katie let herself drift off into a dreamy state, just for a moment. What had the dragon meant about song lines running through the cosmos? Songs must be so important on this world. After all, Za's guardian had given him a journey song to guide them, even if it didn't make much sense. She drowsed, humming a bit under her breath. The spring sang merrily, the bee buzzed happily, and the brown bird repeated three pure notes over and over again. In a way, maybe, it was like the whole world was singing. Or, if the dragon was right, the whole cosmos. Did the stars sing too, each with their own note?

Rubbing her gritty eyes, Katie noticed a new sound. Click click. Click click. Was Za cracking his knuckles? Too tired to open her eyes, she imagined the clicking as part of the interweaving songs. Click click. Louder now. Click click. Buzz buzz. Splish splash. Tap-tap. Chirp cheep cheep. Click click. Why was Za cracking his knuckles so close to her head? She didn't bother to say anything at this latest annoyance. He probably wouldn't quit anyway. Click click CLACK! That was right by her head. She'd have to tell Za to quit and leave her alone so she could rest. She was so tired. And hungry, too. That piece of fruit Za had shared with her hadn't been much. Click click CLACK!

Katie reluctantly opened her eyes.

A massive red lobster claw reached out from below the rock. Katie jerked upright and watched as the claw was followed by antennae and round black eyes. A scorpion—nearly as big as her! Katie leapt off the boulder. "Run!"

Za ducked just in time to miss being pinched, and then hobbled as fast as he could after Katie. The scorpion sped after them both on its hairy legs.

"Hurry, Za!" urged Katie, watching him limp-run. She had to do something. *But what?*

Katie grabbed a large rock and chucked it at the scorpion. The rock bounced right off its hard exoskeleton. The scorpion lashed its long jointed tail at Za, missing him by inches.

Za's infected ankle gave way, and he tripped, landing in a heap.

The scorpion bent in a U, so that its head looked at Za at the same time that the stinging tail hung over him. "I st-st-sting you, my chunky," chittered the scorpion. "My venom will paralyze and preserve you and I can eat you a bit at a time, fresh and living, the way I like my meat."

Katie gripped a long branch and bashed it against one of the scorpion's antennae. For an instant the feeler crumpled, but in a blink it unfurled into its normal shape. The scorpion lowered its stinger to Za's cheek.

"Stop, Stop, Stop! You have to stop!" yelled Katie.

"What is this, my chunky? Does the beastie talk? I don't eat *talking* beasties."

"Yes! Yes! We talk!" screamed Katie, wringing wet and hysterical with fear. "You can't eat us."

The scorpion pulled the stinger back up an inch and looked at Za. "Such a ch-ch-chuicy smell. I hate to miss my meal, but I has principles. Does *this* one talk?" It scrutinized Za with a beady eye.

"Yes, he talks!" yelled Katie, dimly aware of the hedge in back of her snapping and crackling as if another large animal was behind her. But she couldn't take her eyes off the scorpion to look. She felt, superstitiously perhaps, that the second she looked away the scorpion would sting Za.

"I must hear from him," said the scorpion without moving an inch from Za, who already looked paralyzed, probably from fear since he had not yet been stung. Silence hung heavy in the air.

"Say something," cried Katie. "You have to say something!"

"Run Katie," croaked Za, "before it gets you too. If you see my guardian tell him I'm sorry I failed."

"Keep talking!" implored Katie. "It doesn't eat talking animals."

Za inhaled. "How do you know?"

The scorpion lowered its stinger back down to Za's cheek. "*This* chunky one just makes silly squeaks. It is not a talking beastie at all."

"He talks to me!" howled Katie.

"But he doesn't talk to me, now does he?" said the scorpion. "And, he doesn't look like you. Perhaps he is your pet?" it continued, "But that isn't the same thing, now is it? I has principles, but I does eat pets. And this is such a nice meal. Too good to miss. Now I st-st-sting."

"No!" cried Katie, immobilized with fear as she watched the stinger almost penetrate Za's plum-colored skin.

A loud crash rattled the bushes behind Katie and then a roar echoed off the rocks. Kira! Katie quit breathing as she watched the lion charge the scorpion, knocking it away from Za. The scorpion rose on its tail in a fury of clicking and clacking claws.

Katie ran over to Za and dragged him away from the fray.

The giant scorpion and Kira blurred together in a spinning heap of noisy chittering madness. "We've got to do something," sobbed Katie. "What if it gets Kira?"

"Are you crazy?" replied Za. "There's nothing we can do but use this chance to try and get away. Look at them." He pointed. "You can't even see where one ends and the other begins."

"But Kira could die!"

"Do you want her to give her life for nothing?!"

The orange body of the scorpion wrapped around Kira, its tail poised over the lion's head. Kira bit the center of the scorpion's belly, ripping a hole beneath the armor, then leaped away from the deadly tail.

Katie's mind raced. If she threw rocks she might accidentally hit Kira. She couldn't battle the thing, she'd just get in the way. "The lion is a talking beast too!" she lied desperately.

But the scorpion and the lion were so engaged in their snarling clacking fight that they didn't even pause at her words.

"Hurry, Katie," urged Za. "You've got to help me up the trail. This is my only chance. If Kira loses, I'll never be able to run away in time."

Katie gave one last look at the fearless Kira and then she let Za lean on her while they struggled up the mountain. She couldn't bear to lose Kira. Not after already losing home and Mom and Dad and Sasha. With every step she prayed, "Please let Kira win. Por favor, please let Kira win."

Za leaned heavily on Katie's shoulder, panting as the two of them staggered up the steep slope. "The Winged Ones will be at the top, right?" asked Katie.

Za grunted. "Yeah, that's what it sounds like in my journey song."

Katie slipped on some loose rocks, and the two of them stopped talking, using all their energy to concentrate on each step. It would be so easy to fall on this shale and slide all the way back down the mountain.

Katie was so busy looking down at the ground that it surprised her when she crested the slope. They were on top. Vast blue sky surrounded them and not far below, a lake. Nothing else. There were no Winged Ones in sight. Katie's heart sank. "You said they would be here."

She felt like weeping from disappointment, but a sudden rattle of stones drew her attention. Someone was coming up the mountain. Katie clenched her nails into her palm, waiting to see who it was, Kira or the scorpion.

It was covered in red and black blood. Squinting, Katie's heart sank. It looked like the scorpion.

A low, throaty purr emerged from the bloody mess. "Kira!" Katie ran to the lion. "I was so afraid I'd never see you again."

Katie ripped off the hem of her shirt and wiped the blood out of Kira's eyes, examining her for injuries. The wounds didn't look serious—nothing deep. Most of the blood seemed to belong to the scorpion. Thank God. Everything would be better now that Kira was with them again. If only she could talk to the lion. How she longed to ask Kira how she'd beat the scorpion. It didn't make any sense. Why could she talk with the dragon and the scorpion and not Kira?

Za put a tentative hand out and patted the top of Kira's head. He muttered something that sounded like "Thanks" under his breath, and Katie stared at him amazed, wondering if she'd heard right.

"It's not so easy to get rid of me," gibbered the scorpion, coming up the slope. A bloody, clawless arm dangled from its red body, but the tail wagged whole and menacing. "I'll get my st-st-stinger into the nasty beasties, I will."

Za took Katie's hand and pulled her down the steep slope. "To the lake!" As she bounced and slid, Katie was blinded by the dazzling sun reflecting off the surface of the lake.

Katie slipped after Za, scraping holes in her pants as she tumbled out of control down to the lake where she lay, bruised and gasping on the rocky shore. In the distance, she heard the jabber of the scorpion and Kira's low, throaty growl. "Kira!" shouted Katie, hoping the lion would escape before the scorpion engaged her in another battle. Squinting, she stared up at the mountain, but couldn't see Kira or the scorpion. Soon the sounds of their fighting faded away, and Katie couldn't hear anything. Wishing there was something she could do to help the lion, but unable to think of a single thing, Katie sat up on the bristly tufts of grass growing in the sand between boulders and stared at the lake, catching her breath. Slowly, her heartbeat quit drumming in her ears, and she calmed down enough to look around.

The lake was beautiful, bordered by smooth, white granite. Clouds and rocks reflected on the surface of the water, which went from almost turquoise blue along the shore, to cerulean, and then a dark sea blue at the center. It was so clear that she could see little fish swimming above the sand and pebbles at the bottom.

On the far side, the lake basin was forested with healthy green pines. A gentle breeze whispered through their needles, and the outlet creek burbled in little waterfalls cascading down into a series of clear emerald pools. The high pitched whine of a mosquito and the piercing cry of what sounded like a baby eagle all came together in a melodious concert. Every time she paused for a moment on this journey, the whole world seemed to be singing. Katie waved the mosquito away from her face, shaking her head at the ridiculousness of thinking the irritating sound of a mosquito could be part of a musical composition. But, still, there was a way that even the Eeee of the mosquito complimented the sweet sounds around this peaceful lake.

Inhaling the fragrant air, Katie watched an osprey circling lazily overhead. Suddenly, the white bird plummeted down, rising again with a squirming silver fish held in strong talons. Amazing how the bird waited for exactly the right moment and then dove without hesitation. Mom always said timing was so important in music, and it looked like it was in life too, at least for this osprey. As the bird flew off with the fish, Katie noticed something large swimming in the water. "What's that?" she asked Za, pointing.

The two of them stared as whatever it was swam rapidly towards them. "Looks like a person," replied Za.

Katie smiled. A person was exactly what they needed right now. Someone to help them.

As the person swam closer, kicking so hard that the water formed a wake like the one from a boat, Katie noticed a head full of hair so white it matched the reflections of the clouds on the water.

The swimmer pulled almost to shore and rested partly submerged in the water next to them. He was wearing some sort of odd wetsuit around his legs and had a long white beard. "Greetings," he said in a mellow baritone. "Who are you and what brings the two of you to my lake?"

"I'm Katie and this is Za," replied Katie, relieved that they were actually meeting an adult. "Why we're here is actually a long story."

"You can speak to this one too?" whispered Za.

Katie gave him a quick look and then turned back to the man.

His blue eyes lit up. "A story?" he asked. "My name is Seidon, and there's nothing I love more than a good story." He smiled so warmly that Katie immediately felt reassured. Surely he'd help them. "Would you like to come to my dwelling for some refreshment, and you can share your story?"

"We don't have much time," replied Katie. "We have to finish our quest before…"

Seidon raised his bushy white eyebrows. "Surely you need to eat, even on a quest?"

"True," said Katie, who was really hungry. "But we can't stay long."

Seidon reached out with his long arms and tucked her and Za on either side of his body. "What?!" asked Katie, squirming to get free. But Seidon held her firmly, kicked with his wet suited legs, which looked like a giant green fish tail, taking all of them out to the deep water.

"You'll want to take a breath in and hold it," said Seidon.

"Hold your breath!" Katie shouted to Za, gulping in air a second before the fish-man pulled them under the water.

CHAPTER TWELVE

Charmed, I'm sure

Icy water closed over Katie's head. She pushed against Seidon's leathery skin. He held her in an arm the size of an elephant's trunk and they plunged deeper and deeper.

Za, caught in the other arm, stared at Katie with huge yellow eyes. He opened and closed his mouth like a panic-stricken fish, his limbs lashing frantically in all directions. His foot hit Katie's leg. Pain shot up her shin.

A trickle of stale air escaped her lungs. Her pulse pounded against her eardrums. Katie's skin numbed in the cold water. So much for this adult being friendly. What had she been thinking?

Desperate, she opened her mouth and sank her teeth deep into Seidon's arm. Something salty and warm flowed across her tongue. Blood? Katie sputtered and choked. Seidon didn't slow. He only squeezed her more tightly, crushing the last lungful of air out of her.

Black spots swam before Katie's eyes. Her body went limp. *Home. Mom, Dad, Sasha…*

Seidon slowed and opened the door of a beautiful cottage. The windows were ovals of pearly glass set into a house shingled with shells of all sorts: clams, mussels, starfish and sea snails. Even a huge conch hung over the door.

Katie floated effortlessly past it, like a ghost. Was she dead? She looked curiously around the small chamber. A second, inner door opened and, once again, she felt herself propelled forward.

A gust of warm air rushed to meet her. Katie opened her mouth and took a deep breath. A thousand sharp needles pierced her lungs, shooting tingles down her hands and legs. She wasn't dead. A hot wave of relief swept Katie's body. She forced herself to take another breath, to bear the pricking pain of being alive. Looking around the cozy circular room Katie noted the gleaming iridescent couch, wondering what material it was.

Seidon used his powerful arms to drag his huge body across the floor. Katie stared at his legs. That wasn't a wet suit. The lower half of Seidon's body was a fish tail! He wasn't a man after all, but some sort of fish-man. His tail left a wide wet S across the mosaic coral floor. The weight of all the water outside pressed in, making Katie feel trapped. "How come we can breathe down here, way under water?"

"I've created an air chamber," the fish-man said proudly. He curled his tail into a cushion and sat on it.

Katie nodded, relieved, still drinking in the air. "How long are you going to keep us here?"

"That depends on the story," answered the fish-man.

"I don't get why you can understand him when I can't," grumbled Za, pulling the plain brown pebble the dragon had given him out of his pocket and turning it over and over.

Katie glanced at him, the glimmer of an idea poking her stunned mind. There must be a reason why she could understand these creatures when Za, with his gift of tongues, could not.

The fish-man pointed his finger and sent an electrical current to a lamp, which lit immediately. It was made out of some strange see-through material. Not plastic, or glass—more like the inflated body of a jellyfish. "Please sit down and make yourselves at home."

Katie's knees wobbled as she made her way weakly over to the couch, noticing that her clothes were drying quickly in the warm air. She sank gratefully down; observing as she did that the sofa was actually made out of fish skins very cleverly stitched together. She couldn't stop shaking.

"Is there ought else I can do to increase your comfort?"

"Just maybe the food you offered," replied Katie in a small voice. She'd have to stay on Seidon's good side if they were ever going to get out of here. There was no way they'd be able to swim all the way back up to the surface again without his help.

Seidon clapped his hands and a small school of fish flew into the room, carrying shells full of food on their tails. They looked like funny birds flying through the air. After them came a seahorse balancing a pearl on its nose.

Katie watched the tiny creature settle in the fish-man's beard. What kind of magic did Seidon have to keep fish and a seahorse alive in the air?

The smell of soup made Katie's stomach gurgle. It must taste okay since Za was gobbling like crazy. Katie's hands trembled as she lifted the shell bowl of chowder to her lips and sipped. The tasty broth slid down her throat, settling warmly in her stomach.

Za popped and crunched waterweeds between his blue teeth.

After they'd eaten, Seidon handed Katie an abalone shell filled with violet liquid. It was sweet, almost like grape juice, only with a salty aftertaste. "May the waters of life be with you," said the fish-man.

"Thank you," replied Katie.

Seidon looked expectantly at Za, but he kept slurping his soup without looking up. "Is your companion rude that he does not answer my invocation?"

A little giggle burst out of Katie. She couldn't help it. Za *was* so rude sometimes.

"Why are you laughing?" asked Za. "I don't see how you can find *anything* funny about our situation!"

The corners of Katie's mouth turned up in a secret smile as she imagined what Za's expression would be if he understood the fish-man.

"Before you begin your story, I should tell you a bit about myself," said Seidon, stroking his beard. "I have been found on all worlds where there is water since the beginning of life." He leaned back against a cushion, clapping his hands so that the fleet of brilliantly colored fish returned, taking the shell bowls from the driftwood table. Za picked up one last strand of sea grapes before the fish departed through a little round window that led into another room. "I'm looking forward to hearing your tale," added Seidon. "I do hope it is something I haven't heard before." He sniffed. "One of the disadvantages of being around for so long is that most stories are no longer new to me." He fanned his tail slowly back and forth over the floor. "I've been searching all the stories looking for my beloved, who disappeared a long age ago. She used to visit me as siren, selkie and mermaid. I loved to listen to her sing as she combed her long hair." Seidon sighed heavily. "In order for us Water Beings to take form, we need clear clean water that reflects the moon and stars. Then we are all part of one whole and the water expresses the patterns of our songs." Seidon stroked his long beard. "Now the waters of my world are trying to clear something poisonous."

Katie shivered. *This had to be related to the dirty water and hot steam with the horrible voice in the swamp.*

"The worst is," continued the fish-man, "the waters are failing. Instead of clearing the problem, they are becoming toxic themselves so that the frogs and dragonflies seek refuge here, at my lake."

"What's he saying?" asked Za.

Katie shook her head at Za, and said to Seidon, "I did notice there wasn't much life in the marsh."

"I only hope my beloved is safe and hasn't been caught in those foul waters."

Seidon looked so sad that Katie wished she could help him, but she knew her story had nothing to do with this fish-man or his lost love. "I hate to disappoint you," said Katie, "but I doubt our story will be new." She leaned forward hopefully. "Why don't you avoid wasting your time, and just take us back up?"

"I must hear your story first and then I'll be the judge," said Seidon.

Katie's heart sank. She nervously twisted her charm bracelet around and around. Then she stopped. Seidon's face stared up at her from one of the charms—the one that had reminded her of a grumpy Santa Claus. The dragon, the scorpion, and the fish-man; they were all charms. That was the magic of the bracelet. It let her speak with the ones shown on the charms!

Seidon interrupted her thoughts with a piercing look. "Let the story begin. If it is an interesting tale, I will help you return to the surface."

Katie gulped. She'd have to tell it *all*, since Za couldn't talk to him, and she *wasn't* a very good storyteller. No one ever laughed at her jokes. Besides, how could her story entertain Seidon, when he himself had said that he'd already heard most stories? *Would he keep them here* forever *if she bored him?*

CHAPTER THIRTEEN

A Dirty Trick

Katie began her story in a tiny voice. "We aren't from this world. It all started when…"

Seidon held his hand up. "What kind of story is this, told in plain everyday words? Stories are meant to be sung! The bards of old always told their tales in rhymes and song."

Katie swallowed hard. "I don't think I can sing it," she said.

"Nonsense," replied Seidon. "The universe is made of songs. One verse to create them all. And all comes together in one united verse. Really everything is song, when we have the ears to hear. I'm sorry I don't have a harp to accompany you. But you must do your best to sing your story."

Katie started over, singing about the earthquake.

"When I was home alone, an earthquake
made my whole bedroom shake and shake,
I fell down through a giant crack
And landed on my head with a smack,
Everything whirled and twirled and swirled
Until I saw Za between the worlds."

Her rhymes were rough and lacked rhythm, but what could Seidon expect off the top of her head? Good thing she and Mom always made silly songs out of everyday life or she wouldn't have been able to do it at all. Katie inhaled, ready to begin the next stanza when Seidon held his hand up again for her to stop. He asked her what an earthquake was and then, when she'd explained—this time not in song, which seemed to be okay with him as long as she was answering questions and not telling the actual story—he wanted to know what she meant about Za being between worlds.

After she explained about Za traveling from world to world, Seidon barked out a scoffing laugh. "How can you expect me to believe that your idiot friend who doesn't even have common courtesy is capable of inter-world travel?"

"But, Za's not really an idiot."

"An idiot!" howled Za. "That beast dares call me, Za, an IDIOT?" Za shoved the pebble back in his pocket and paced around the room on his infected ankle like a trapped and wounded bear.

Seidon gave an irritated flick of his tail. "I can do something with him if he's bothering you."

"No thanks," Katie answered quickly.

"You should choose your companions more wisely," advised Seidon. "This Za leaves something to be desired, especially in terms of manners."

"Yes, well," said Katie, thinking that she hadn't been given much choice of companions. Then she returned to something that had been troubling her. "You know, I traveled between worlds too."

"I'm curious about that," said Seidon, tugging on his beard. "It's unlikely an earth imbalance would send you to another world," he mused, "unless there was already huge imbalance in your life." Seidon held up his white hands with their smooth, tapered fingers. Instead of nails, they were tipped with blue-green scales. "It's possible you are needed here in this world to help somehow."

Katie's muscles tensed. Dania had said she might be sent to help. "What could I possibly have to offer?"

Seidon's face clouded. "I don't know, but there is that malignant presence fouling the waters of this world and I suspect many others. Perhaps…" Seidon shook himself, as if banishing his pensive mood. "I see you are using an old trick," he said sternly, "asking questions so that I talk instead of you getting on with your story." He scowled. "Sing me your tale."

Katie drew in a deep breath of the stale, fishy smelling air.

"Yes there was imbalance in my home,
and that is what caused me to roam.
My parents had a terrible fight,
and it gave me quite a big fright.
They had promised to get me a horse,
for my coming birthday of course…"

"A horse?" asked Seidon. "What is this?"

"Horses are the most wonderful animals in the world," said Katie, relieved to answer a question without having to rhyme or sing. "They are beautiful, and I can ride on their backs, and they always seem to know how I'm feeling."

"I see," Seidon nodded sagely. "They are like dolphins or, for someone of my magnificent size, whales."

Katie tucked a tendril of hair back into her messy braid. "Not exactly. They have four legs and they live on land. Anyway, when I turned eleven, my parents said I couldn't have one after all because we have to sell the house and live in two smaller houses where there won't be room for a horse." She swallowed hard. "All because they've decided to get a divorce." Katie bit her lip. "I was so mad that I slammed the door and yelled at them and did something even worse..." Katie hung her head, too embarrassed to share the words she'd shouted at Mom and Dad. "At the time, I didn't think that I was going to fall into another world and maybe never see them again."

Seidon ran his fingers through his beard. "How differently we would live our lives if we but knew the future in advance."

Katie barely heard him. Now that she was talking about it at last, it felt like a dike had burst and the words gushed out in a flood. "So Mom said that I could stay home and cool off while she gave some music lessons, and then my friend Amy came over but she left before the earthquake and and..."

"You are no storyteller," interrupted Seidon. "I will give you one more chance."

Katie swallowed the rest of her tears in one gulp and began singing again.

> *"In the basement I could not see,*
> *and I did not know just how to flee,*
> *until I met Za..."*

"What is this basement?" inquired Seidon.

Katie explained, wishing that he wouldn't ask so many questions. It was hard to keep her thoughts straight when he kept interrupting constantly. After Seidon was finally satisfied that he understood what a basement was, Katie continued with the story, trying to sing, rhyme and make her meeting with Dania as entertaining as possible.

"Dania is beauty with smooth skin,
wearing green leaves, she feels like kin."

"What was Dania's abode like?"

"It was made from living trees."

"What did she eat?" asked Seidon, sounding excited. "How did she live? Were there any waters nearby?"

"I can only answer one question at a time," said Katie, wondering for an instant if maybe Dania was Seidon's long lost beloved. But it didn't make sense that a fish-man who lived under water would be with a woman who couldn't leave the forest.

"Fine, but get on with your story."

Katie swallowed around her parched throat. "Can Za and I have something to drink first?"

Seidon had the fish bring in more of the bubbling violet drinks, but he kept on asking questions. "Why didn't Dania come with you? Where is her forest?"

Katie took a sip from her shell cup and answered the question without singing, "Dania's forest is on the other side of the marsh."

"You already told him that," whispered Za.

"Shh!" hissed Katie.

"We'll never finish the quest on time if you insist on repeating the same details over and over to this fish!" As if for emphasis, Za gave an angry swat at a turquoise fish flying by. The platter on its tail clanked to the floor.

"My fish!" boomed Seidon. He pointed his finger at Za and spun an electrical web of blue light around him.

Za stumbled on his injured leg and fell against the bars of light. The room filled with the sickening smell of sizzling flesh.

"Let him out right now!" yelled Katie. "Can't you see he has a hurt leg and can't stand for long?"

"I'm tired of him interrupting the story." Seidon glowered, for the first time looking as grumpy as the old man on her charm bracelet.

"Listen," said Katie, surprised at her own stern tone, "I'm not going to tell you the story if you don't let him go."

Seidon glanced at the turquoise fish, still wavering around the spilled plate. He picked up the fish and checked it carefully before letting it go into the air. "Za is lucky. My fish is only a bit dazed, not hurt." He motioned with his hand and Za's cage disappeared.

Katie breathed again. She knew it was pressing her luck, but she asked anyway. "Can you do something to fix his leg?"

"Maybe," replied Seidon, pointing at Za, who was pushing and pushing against the outer door, "but why bother? He really is a ridiculous creature."

This time Seidon's put-down of Za didn't make Katie giggle. "Maybe you should let him go, while I stay here and finish the story?"

"I'm sorry, but I cannot," said Seidon. "It might harm the pattern. Together you arrived, and together you shall go." Seidon dragged himself to the door, calling over his shoulder, "If Za hurts the fish or interrupts the story again he will have to spend the rest of the visit in my blue cage." Seidon opened the door and went out, letting it fall shut behind him.

"Don't interrupt," warned Katie, giving Za a serious look, "or Seidon will cage you."

Za held up his arm so that Katie could see the burn on his wrist. "I'll fry!"

"Well it was stupid to hit his fish," said Katie.

"Don't you think I know that?" Za pulled the pebble from his pocket. "I was hoping this was a magic pebble but clearly it's not," he said, kicking the driftwood table. "Darn! Now both legs hurt." He slumped onto the sofa. "I wish I could do something to get us out of here, but I can't even talk to him."

"You'll have to trust me," said Katie, feeling her heart soften as she watched Za and noticed how small and young he looked. "Seidon said he'd help us return to the surface if he likes my story."

Za raised his head. "Tell him…"

Seidon blasted in, carrying a dozen, squirming white things with little suckers on their bellies. "These will drink the poison."

Katie explained that to Za while Seidon attached the suckers onto his leg. Za grimaced, but he sat perfectly still.

"Now tell me what happened after you left Dania's forest," ordered Seidon.

"Dania could not come with us,
which was the very worst sort of fuss.
Only in the forest she exists,
and then she vanished in the mists."

"Definitely not my love, then," remarked Seidon, "but she could be one of the tree spirits. I have heard of them and their shape-shifting ways."

"What is a tree spirit?" asked Katie.

"Please, no more sidetracking me with questions," said Seidon. "Where did you go when you left the forest?"

"We went into the wet marshy bog,
where there was not even a frog."

Katie's voice sounded hoarse as she continued singing, her rhymes getting worse and worse as she described Za falling into the filthy water.

"That is when Za took a big bad hit,
and the slimy marsh creature bit."

"I wouldn't have fallen if Kira hadn't scared me," Za mumbled.

Katie shot him a please shut up, you're-going-to-get-us-in-trouble look.

"In mire Za would have been lost,
but Kira came and out he was tossed."

Seidon frowned. "Strange behavior for an animal, unless Kira is Dania's familiar."

Katie knew better than to ask what a familiar was. She continued on, singing as best she could even though her throat felt raw, telling about the dragon, the emerald, and escaping the marsh. She mentioned the fog-fiends and then sang the name of the Poison One under her breath in a bare whisper. Mentioning the name gave her a strange sense of foreboding, almost as if just naming it could attract the attention of whatever it was that lay in wait for her.

Her voice was raspy by the time she reached the part about the scorpion. That didn't seem to bother Seidon. He made her go on, barely allowing her time to eat or drink. Finally, when her voice gave out completely, he got up to leave the room, calling over his shoulder as he left, "You can sleep now."

Katie curled up gratefully on the smooth couch.

As soon as she shut her eyes, Za said, "Katie, wake up. I have a plan."

Katie opened her stinging eyes. She was so tired. But if Za had a plan to escape…

"You can talk to him," continued Za, watching the white suckers, now three times their original size, plop off his leg onto the floor. "Maybe he'll let us go if you tell him we're on an important quest."

Katie rolled herself into a tight ball and muttered, "You don't understand. There's no way he's going to free us until I finish telling a story that doesn't bore him."

"You have to persuade him. Tell him that our quest will help his world, but only if we hurry. Remember, my guardian said I only have until the third moon wanes."

"What happens if you haven't finished the quest by then?" asked Katie. "Does your guardian come and get you and then make you do your initiation over again somewhere else?"

"No!" cried Za. "If I fail, I fail. I could be stuck on this world for the rest of my life!"

A shiver went down the back of Katie's neck. She could feel the little hairs rising. Deep down, she'd believed that if they didn't finish on time, Za's guardian would come and take him home, and her as well.

Seidon returned dripping wet from the other room. "Since you are up and talking, you will resume the story. How did you escape the scorpion?"

Katie gave Za a reproachful look. She felt so exhausted that she could barely think, and now he'd robbed her of her chance to sleep. "Kira saved us," she began wearily, forgetting to sing.

"Sing!" reminded Seidon, "And tell me what happened to Kira. Did the stinger get her? Was she wounded?"

Katie inhaled, reaching desperately for a rhyme.

"Kira was definitely hurt,
by the scorpion's deadliest squirt."

Inwardly, Katie groaned. Squirt was really reaching as it had been more of a sting. But she was so tired. It was harder and harder to come up with any rhyming words at all. She sang on as best she could, describing the battle, the way the scorpion looked, and their escape.

"I don't know if Kira lives still,
but she is brave and fights with a will."

Katie's song trailed off completely.

"Go on," prodded Seidon.

"That's the end," replied Katie. "Afterwards we ran down to the lake to escape the scorpion and we met you." She forced herself to meet Seidon's penetrating gaze. "Did you like my story?"

Seidon regarded her with a happy twinkle in his blue eyes. "Not bad," he said at last. "There was no sign of my lost beloved in it, but I must admit I've never heard a story quite like it."

Katie leaned forward. "You weren't bored?"

"Not at all," said Seidon, smiling. "I found it rather entertaining."

A wave of relief swept over Katie. "You promised to take us back to the surface if you liked my story."

"True," agreed Seidon, tucking his tail more comfortably beneath him, "but I never said when."

CHAPTER FOURTEEN

A Difficult Decision

Katie jumped up. “We have to finish our quest before the third moon wanes!”

Seidon shrugged.

“What about the Poison One I told you about?” asked Katie, her voice quavering as she spoke its name. She had to persuade Seidon, no matter what it took, but Katie cringed as something eager in the back of her mind woke up and pounced. “Yesss,” it hissed, “What about me?”

Seidon’s forehead furrowed into a deep frown. “It is possible the Poison One in your story is the same entity responsible for sickening the waters.”

“You said that maybe I was sent to this world to help somehow. Dania thought so too. Perhaps it’s by stopping the…the…,” she couldn’t bear to speak its name aloud again, “you know, whatever is harming the waters. It may be making its way to your lake now! If you don’t let us go then it will spread!” Katie knew she was reaching, wasn’t sure if this was true, but it was possible and she had to talk Seidon into letting them go.

“Nice argument,” whispered Za.

Electric sparks flew off Seidon’s head. Katie could see she’d made an impression, but she wasn’t sure if it was convincing. “I do sense the contamination in the waters expanding,” he growled. “Unfortunately, you can’t leave now. The surface of my lake has frozen.”

“That can’t be!” wailed Katie. “When we arrived, the flowers were blooming. It was spring!”

“Time passes differently under the lake,” replied Seidon, plucking a blue fish from the air and stroking it absently with his thumb. “You have been here longer than you know. Once the lake freezes, it usually remains so until at least one of the moons is full in the sky.”

Sweat trickled down Katie’s back. “Have all the moons waned?”

“No. A half-moon remains.”

Za pulled Katie’s arm. “What did he say? Are we too late?”

Katie put a finger to her lips. “Shhh.” Then she asked Seidon, “There must be some way to get through the ice. Surely you, with your great strength, could break a hole for us?”

Seidon glowered. “How dare you ask me to commit such an act of violence?”

“You misunderstood,” said Katie, cringing. *Why did he look so angry*? “I don’t want you to hurt anyone—just to break a hole in the ice.”

“It is *you* who misunderstands,” roared Seidon. “My lake is not some inanimate object that you can just attack, breaking her ice! She is a conscious being in her own right and deserves to be asked if she is willing to melt.” A storm of sparks showered off him.

One landed on Za’s leg.

Seidon flapped his moist fin against Za’s thigh and put the flame out. He added casually, “My beautiful lake will decide in her own time when to melt.”

Katie’s mind raced. “The lake is conscious?”

"Of course, you silly-legged creature. I am king of this lake. I used to be king of all waters, and I can tell you they are conscious, intelligent and aware."

Katie's pulse leapt, almost as if for an instant the crystal water Dania had given her sang in her veins.

"When worlds were new, I lived in every drop, spring, creek, river, waterfall, lake, and ocean, floating in bliss. I inhabited all beings in the water that ran through them." A sunny glow lit Seidon's face. Then he resumed his all-too-frequent frown. "Alas, although I continue to sense the other waters, they have gone their own ways. Many are now polluted, and I can't reach them."

"I'm sorry," said Katie, remembering the filthy swamp water.

He looked so gloomy that Katie tried to comfort him. "At least you have this lake."

Seidon groaned. "Not for long, if the pollution keeps spreading."

Katie took her chance. "The pollution must be coming from…you know," she winced. "Dania told us the birds think the marsh waters are being fouled by it, and you speak of the waters' inability to clear something terrible. Then there's what I saw and heard in the marsh. It's all connected and must be what's causing this mess." She pulled on her braid and then added firmly, "Za and I have a chance to stop it." Katie was careful not to tell Seidon how slim that chance actually was as she pressed her point. "That's why you have to let us go."

Seidon gave her one of his long, measuring looks. "You can go on one condition: you must prove that you are in harmony with my lake by asking her to melt the ice."

"Me!" exclaimed Katie, and then, when she'd recovered from the shock of his absurd request, she added, "Can't you help? I mean, since you're the king of the lake, and you float in bliss and all, couldn't you just get the ice to melt?" She fiddled with her braid. "It'd only be for a few minutes. Just long enough for us to get out."

Seidon continued to stroke the blue fish. "Of course the lake would probably melt for me, but that isn't the point. You'll have to do this on your own, with the help of *him*," he said pointing at Za, "although it's hard for me to see what benefit he'll be."

"But, why?" cried Katie, frantic. "Don't you *want* us to get away so we can stop the…?"

Seidon lifted his shoulders in a careless shrug. "If you are indeed the one sent, then you will be able to melt the ice. Otherwise, I don't see much point in letting you go."

"What if I fail to melt the ice?" squeaked Katie. "Will you come and get us?"

Seidon gently released the blue fish into the air. "If you can't melt the ice then, most likely, you will die. Your bones will sink into the bottom of the lake nourishing waterweeds and fish and in that way you will become part of them, continuing on in different life forms."

"But not as us," said Katie. The room was perfectly quiet except for the soft swish-swish of fish-fins flapping in the air. "I don't want to be a fish!"

Za's eyes widened. "What's going on? Can he turn us into fish?"

Katie explained everything to Za. "What should we do?" she asked. "We could die!"

"We'll die anyway if we get stuck on this world," Za said flatly. "We have no way to live and think of all the dangerous animals we've already met. Who knows what else is out there."

Katie nodded. Za was right.

Seidon cleared his throat. "Well, what's it to be?"

"Can't you at least tell me how to ask the lake?" Katie cleared her throat. "What should I do?"

"Why, you must talk to the lake, of course," replied Seidon, clapping his hands for a drink.

"How?" asked Katie, looking down at her charm bracelet. There was no charm of anything like a lake, or even a drop of water. "I can't talk to a lake!"

"The one clue I'll give you is something the ocean once told me long ago, in the days when I could merge with all waters." His stormy sea-blue eyes dimmed with a faraway expression. "She said that there is something common that connects all beings."

Katie's foot jiggled up and down. "What does that mean?"

Seidon looked up. "You'll have to find the answer yourself. Are you ready to try to melt the ice?"

No, thought Katie, but she felt her head, almost involuntarily, nod 'Yes'.

Seidon quickly flicked the latch on the door with the edge of his fin, then clutched each of them under one of his arms and dragged them out the door.

"Wait!" screamed Katie, trying to wriggle out of Seidon's arm. "I need another clue!" she burbled as a wave of cold water washed over her.

Seidon shot up to the top of the lake. Water streamed around them in a white froth. It grew brighter as they neared the surface until Katie saw opaque light shining through the ice. This time, Katie clung to Seidon, but he wriggled free and left her and Za alone underneath the ice. With one strong wave of his tail, he dove back down into the depths.

CHAPTER FIFTEEN

Why Didn't I Notice Before?

Katie swam around, desperately looking for an opening. She pushed against the ice. It didn't give. *Oh, God.*

Za pounded frantically on the impenetrable frozen ceiling.

No use. The ice stretched in one clear hard sheet across the lake.

Have to talk to the lake, remembered Katie. How? Maybe in her mind. *Dear Lake,* Katie mentally begged, *please melt. We mean no harm. Let us go.*

The frozen water remained as solid and cold as ever. Her lungs screamed for air. *Think fast.*

Ringing ears. *Hard to think. Have to think. Find what connects all beings.* A picture series went through Katie's mind: riding horses, Sasha curled in the sun, Mom reading her stories, Amy's smiling face, and Dad's bear hugs. *What connects us?*

Za swam up fast, bashing his head against the ice. He didn't even make a dent, but his body went limp and started sinking, down into the depths.

Katie used her last energy, diving down, down. Grabbing Za. Holding his flaccid body in her arms, kicking hard, back up, up, towards the light.

A spasm twisted Za's body. He opened his yellow eyes, swam away and then back again to attack the ice.

Katie's body squirmed in breathless agony. She pressed up against the ice. *Melt! Melt! Melt!* Weak. Dizzy. Black stars floated in front of her eyes. She lay back, defeated. *Can't do it.*

The last air seeped out of her lungs as she floated languidly in the water. Nothing seemed important anymore except for the luminous way the light shone through the ice. Katie rocked gently in the water so that it was hard to tell where her body ended and the lake began. The rhythm of the holy spring water in her body, her blood, her cells, and the fluid in her spine flowed in harmony with that of the lake. Calmly, softly, as if she'd always known, it came to her: *Water! Water is an element shared by all life.*

Peace filled her heart. No need to hurry. No need to escape. Life. Death. Life. All one watery flow. She could linger longer here in this simple bliss of being. Rays of sunshine split into separate shafts, shining in the water, making the fish gleam rainbow colors. *And sunshine. Fire. Warmth. Another element. And air. There was something about air.* A few bubbles escaped her mouth and she watched them float away, enchanted at their slow motion drift. It no longer seemed so important that she could not remember whatever it was about air.

Za shoved something hard into her palm and pressed her fingers around it. Opening her hand Katie stared down at the dragon's pebble. *Earth. Didn't she need to get back to Earth? But the water was so beautiful, so tranquil, so welcoming.* Her limp body floated as a wave of sleepiness soothed her system. *All the elements, together,* the thought drifted in her drowsy mind as she began to sink. *All the elements together. That's what gives life. Life, so amazing, so mysterious. We're all made out of the elements and in that way we're all connected, all one.*

Suddenly, Za tugged on her arm. *Distracting.* Katie wished he'd leave her alone to enjoy these last precious moments. He kicked, pulling her up with him. She was too tired and lethargic to resist. Was he going to try to pound through again?

Her head popped out of the water.

"You did it, Katie!" exclaimed Za. "You melted the ice!"

Katie coughed and coughed. Finally, she inhaled a bit of the sweet air. "But, all I did was think."

"I saw it happen!" Za shouted. "You got a funny look on your face and all of a sudden the ice melted and now we're here."

Katie looked around for the first time. "Here?" It didn't look anything like the lake she'd entered. This lake was set in a green meadow. Katie swam to shore and pulled herself onto the grassy bank. Wondrous scents wafted on the breeze. "Where are the boulders?"

"Who cares?" asked Za. "I can see houses at the other end of this field. Maybe the Winged Ones are there."

Katie squinted, but, of course, she couldn't see any houses, only flowers of every hue blooming in all directions: bright sunflowers, daisies, and tiny blue forget-me-nots. Rose and iris and delphiniums. Chrysanthemums and dahlias.

"Come on," said Za

"Let me catch my breath," replied Katie, who wanted a moment to admire the flowers. She handed Za back the pebble. "This helped."

Za pocketed it. "I couldn't think of anything else to do."

"Maybe it *is* a magic pebble," said Katie. "Made me remember earth."

Za ran around in a circle, doing cartwheels and handstands. "Seidon's suckers worked," he chortled happily. "My ankle is better."

Katie slowly stood, panting heavily so that she wouldn't pass out.

"Here," said Za, standing next to her. "Lean on me."

Katie felt grateful for the support even if he was more than a foot shorter than she was. Somehow his hand at her back kept her up as they staggered into the sunny meadow. With every step, her spirits lifted. *We did it. We're here. Maybe I'll really get home after all!*

Birds flew across the sky and warm sunbeams caressed her shoulders. It didn't seem long before she saw the houses. They were such bright colors: ruby red, brilliant yellow, blue and purple. Katie let go of Za and sped up now that their goal was in sight.

A few yards further, a cloud of butterflies surrounded them so thickly that Katie couldn't see. Soft wings beat against the back of her neck, gently nudging her and Za towards the village.

As quickly as they had come, the butterflies dispersed, leaving them standing in the center of the houses. Now that she was here, Katie saw that the "houses" were actually made of enormous flowers, the size of a child's playhouse. She reached her hand out and touched a petal-silk pink wall.

A small person, half Katie's size, appeared in the doorway. She opened her mouth, and the air was filled with song. "Good day," she sang, tossing her many-colored hair away from her face. "Who might you be?"

"I'm Katie, and this is Za. Who are you?"

"Why, I'm Allura of course. I should have thought that was evident. But, no matter. Welcome to the land of flowers."

"Thank you," said Za.

Katie gave him a curious look. "You can understand her, and you don't have the charm!"

Za laughed. "Do you think that charm bracelet is the reason you've understood all these creatures?"

"Of course," answered Katie, noticing more people emerging from their flower houses.

Za wiggled his toes. "Guardian gifts never work unless it's a talent you already have, although they do strengthen those." Za smiled wryly. "I guess that's why I didn't understand all the animals, even with my gift of tongues; I don't really like most animals," he confessed, smiling and nodding his head in the direction of Allura. "But they look just like little people with wings."

For the first time, Katie noticed that the small people each had a pair of gossamer wings, fluttering in the breeze. She grinned happily. "Hooray, we've found you!"

"You must be the Winged Ones," added Za more seriously.

Allura laughed merrily. "We are no such thing."

"You have to be!" cried Katie. "You each have wings!"

"Nonsense," Allura stated firmly, her violet eyes twinkling. "One has to be only what one is, and we are something else entirely."

"Fairies?" asked Katie, thinking that they looked just like the one on her charm.

All the little people laughed at once and the sound was like bells. "Silly folk call us that sometimes."

"You must be special indeed to have found us," she added. "Which gate did you come through?

Za tapped his right foot on the grass. “We didn’t come through a gate.”

“Of course you came through a gate,” sang Allura, who seemed to act as spokeswoman. The four gates are the only way to get into this land.”

“I didn’t see a gate,” said Katie.

Allura nodded wisely. “Sometimes folks don’t. You see, the gates move around, and they aren’t always open. In this land, the flowers blooming above open gates can be any color, but they all take on a wavering shimmer, like a heat mirage. Pay attention when you notice these slight distortions in the air. They are time-space warps and can suck you into quite another place. Be warned, not all of them are friendly places one might wish to visit.” Allura picked up a smooth rock and tossed it towards a fuchsia, orchid-like flower. The air around the rock wavered, and then there was a little sucking sound and both the rock and the flower vanished.

“Where did they go?” asked Za.

Allura shrugged. “Hard to say where the other end of this gate is. We devas are immune to the pull of the gates,” Allura laughed merrily. “Too light and airy, I suppose. Or too much a part of our land. In any case, we never leave our gardens.” Allura gave a wave of her hand, indicating her blooming domain. “Anyway,” she continued more seriously, “back to my question. Since you don’t know which gate you came through, can you tell me where you were before you arrived?”

“We were under the ice in Seidon’s lake, and when it melted we were here,” Katie said simply.

Allura adjusted the crown of flowers she wore on her glittery hair. “Well then, that’s fine.” She smiled, showing her round pearly teeth. “You came through the gate of balance. We chase away anyone who comes through the fuming gate, you know."

Katie sat down and stared into Allura's merry eyes. "How could we have come through the gate of balance?"

"Perhaps you and your companion form a balance, a completion of sorts, or oneness?" suggested Allura.

"No!" shrieked Katie and Za at the same time and for once they were in perfect agreement.

Allura fluttered into the air. "Then you must have become in balance and one with the lake."

Katie nodded slowly. "I saw how we are all made from the elements and are one in that way. The water, the sun, the air…but I'd forgotten the earth until Za reminded me with his pebble."

"Ahh," said Allura. "Can I see your pebble, Za?"

Za took the smooth brown stone out of his pocket and handed it to Allura. She studied it carefully. "Humble and ordinary, like you." She smiled warmly at Za.

Za took his pebble back. "I'm not ordinary!"

The fairies twittered. "He's not ordinary!" said the peach-colored fairy.

"He doesn't understand how extraordinary the ordinary is," added a pink fairy.

"The miraculous beauty of the simple," said the smallest fairy.

"Pay attention to anything and you will see," added Allura. "A worm, a snail, a leaf, a spider spinning—all as ordinary as you."

"You are the silliest creatures I have ever met," Za grumbled. "But what should I expect from a bunch of fairies?!"

The fairies voices pealed together as they chuckled and chimed, tinkling like a set of fine bells. Allura's porcelain cheeks dimpled. "The two of you must be hungry after such an accomplishment." She blew a reed whistle. "Come. We shall feast you."

Immediately, fairies dashed into flower houses, returning with baskets full of food.

"We don't have time for this," said Za, pointing at the daytime sky, where half of one moon was visible. "I have to finish my quest before that moon wanes."

Allura tilted her head back, looking up at Za and laughing musically. "Hurrying won't get you there faster."

"Be like a leaf in the wind," quipped a blue fairy.

"A butterfly on a breeze," added a yellow one.

"Fly on the wings of your dreams and you will find your heart's desire."

"We already know our heart's desire," interjected Katie, her eyes fixed on the half moon. "We have to find the Winged Ones and get home."

"Impossible," giggled an orange fairy, shaking with laughter.

"Have you heard?" asked the green fairy. "She wants to find the Winged Ones."

"Ridiculous," sang a third.

And then, all the fairies tittered and tinkled, fluttering and flitting into the sky, and then flopping back down on the grass where they rolled and rolled, holding their stomachs with mirth. "They think they can *find* the Winged Ones!"

CHAPTER SIXTEEN

Fairy Dreams

Za knelt down so that he looked directly into Allura's eyes. "If we can't find the Winged Ones, how *can* we reach them?"

"Please help us," Katie pleaded.

Allura smiled sweetly. "The question is, can you help yourselves? You see, reality is what you dream."

Like little echoes, or musical afterthoughts, the fairies took up the refrain: "Reality is what you dream. Dream your reality."

The green fairy hovered close to Katie's ear and whispered, "To dream any reality you choose, set the wings of your desire in the winds of possibility."

"I don't have wings," said Katie, growing increasingly frustrated with this fairy nonsense, "Even if I did, what you're saying doesn't make sense."

"She wants sense," chortled the green fairy.

"Sense of smell?" asked a daffodil yellow fairy.

"Sense of taste? Sense of hearing? Sense of touch? Sense of sight?" They all chimed at once. "What is this sense you want?"

"Ohhhh!" Katie cried out in exasperation.

"Calm down," Za said sharply. "We'll never get anywhere this way."

"A very keen observation," noted Allura, flicking her transparent wing. "Not that you'll ever get anywhere any other way, since there is absolutely nowhere to get, all places being the same, and but an illusion." She finished with a proud nod, as if she had said something very wise and important. "Now, come. As I said before, we will feast you. Let it never be said that we lacked in hospitality." She turned and headed down the lightly trodden path of pressed grass that led into the center of the flower village.

Za gave Katie a doubtful look.

Katie shrugged. "I don't think they'll hurt us."

"But, we don't have time to waste."

"Do you have any other ideas about what we should do?" asked Katie, adding softly, "Besides, I'm starved."

"You're always hungry," grumbled Za.

"We've been getting a lot of exercise lately," said Katie, annoyed that Za rarely needed to eat and never seemed to use the bathroom while she was forced to hide in the bushes and relieve herself whenever she had the chance.

Feather soft wings caressed her shoulders as groups of fairies surrounded them. The fairies gently pressed them towards a large pavilion in the center of the village. It was almost the size of a real house, and seemed to be made out of more than one type of flower. The cathedral ceiling resembled stained glass, with light streaming through the flower walls in various colors. In the middle of the room stood a rectangular table of solid silver. Katie admired the etched carvings of flowers and vines that seemed to grow right up the table's legs. Settling herself beside Za on many small satiny cushions, she watched as fairies arranged food from one end of the table to the other. There were fruits of all kinds, and pies, and nut pastries, and bubbling drinks, and breads, and plates of mushrooms steeped in burgundy sauce. Katie's mouth watered. Her stomach gurgled as she loaded her plate. She bit hungrily into a piece of bread.

Everyone stared at her with expressions of mild reproof. No one else was eating.

Katie swallowed quickly, "Is something wrong?"

Allura fixed her enchanting eyes on Katie. "We always thank the Song Seed before we enjoy this world's bounty."

Katie looked down at her plate, embarrassed.

Allura held her hands out to the fairies on either side of her, and they did the same, until there was a chain of hands linked around the table. Katie held Za's long fingers as lightly as possible in her right hand. She marveled at the smooth feel of tiny fairy fingers enclosed in her left hand. All the fairies began to hum, a glorious sound that filled the hall. They sang about the joy of the growing things, the sap flowing in the trees, the roots of shrubs digging into the soil, the green leaf bending towards the sun.

Katie drifted away with the music, until she felt herself a bud waiting to burst into bloom, a shoot growing strong in the soil, a creature of earth and water and sun.

And then suddenly it all stopped and Katie was jolted back to the present, a bit dazed. Allura smiled at her, as if nothing special had happened, and said, "Now, you may eat," in the most ordinary and friendly way.

Katie took a sip of the bubbling pink liquid.

"It isn't often that we have company these days," said Allura. "Folk seem to have forgotten all about us and they take for granted the miracle of the growing things." She smiled warmly. "We are delighted to have you with us."

All down the table, the little people showed their agreement by lifting their goblets and cheering. "To our guests. May you be long with us."

Za choked. "We can't stay long. We have to leave as soon as this meal is over."

"That's right," agreed Katie, picking up a piece of juicy melon with her tiny silver fork. "If we don't leave soon, we'll never be able to make it back to our worlds."

"You may leave, of course," hummed Allura. "We never keep anyone in our land who does not wish to stay."

"Most wish to stay," chorused the other fairies. "Where else could all their dreams come true?"

"My dream is to go home," murmured Katie, but her eyelids felt heavy and it was hard to keep them open.

"Only one of your dreams," sang the funny little people. "We each have many desires, many dreams…"

Katie's body sagged back against the comfortable cushions. *Odd to feel so full, when I've eaten only a few bites.* But she was so tired. *Just a few minutes to rest*, she told herself. *It's been such a long day.*

She drifted into a dream: riding bareback on a beautiful mare across fields of flowers. Amy rode beside her, laughing. She could smell the flowers, taste the wind. "Watch this!" cried Katie, as her horse leapt over a ravine.

She was distracted from her dream by the ticklish feeling of many pairs of small hands under her back. Katie opened her eyes for an instant, and saw that it was the fairies, carrying her. They brought her inside one of the flower houses and laid her gently down on a bed of petals. Katie smiled as she sniffed the sweet fragrance, letting her eyes close, returning to her dream.

The dream shifted, and she was home again with Mom and Dad, the three of them together, laughing, happy, eating popcorn and watching a movie, just the way it used to be before all the unhappiness. Part of her watched herself dream, thinking, *If only I could make it this way again.* Dad scratched her back, and Katie gave him a hug.

Someone shook her. "Wake up, Katie. You've been asleep for days."

Katie opened her eyes and looked vaguely at Za. The walls and ceiling of the flower house looked like a rose-colored, silk tent. She didn't quite fit; her feet stuck out the opening.

"Please, Katie, you have to wake up!"

"Can't..." mumbled Katie.

"This is the bed of petals in my journey song. You have to wake!"

Katie yawned. "What?"

"Remember the journey song!" Za began to sing.

Three moons glow
On golden hills
Lake below
With songs and trills
Brings deep dreams
On petal beds
So it seems
Wake sleepy heads
Together seen
Winged Ones are
Flying serene
Home, home star

He stopped. "Don't you see, Katie? You're on a bed of petals, we got here from underneath a lake, and now the fairy songs have put you to sleep. If you wake, we'll find the Winged Ones."

"Maybe," murmured Katie, stretching sleepily, "but right now I'm so tired, and I'm in the middle of the best dream." She rolled back over.

"No!" cried Za. "You have to get up now!"

"Why don't you go find the Winged Ones first," she murmured. "Come back for me."

"Wake up!" Za said gruffly.

"Ten more minutes…" murmured Katie, wondering why he was making such a big deal about a little nap. Her eyes closed again. The grey mare pawed impatiently, waiting for her.

Something gripped Katie's ankles and yanked, hurting her back. She was pulled off her soft petal bed, out of her shelter, and bumped over the uneven ground. Once again, Katie forced sleepy eyes open. "Stop dragging me!"

"Don't you understand?" asked Za. "We have to leave *now*, while they're asleep. Otherwise, they'll send us back into dreams, and we won't ever get out of here."

"Who will send us?"

"The fairies," whispered Za. "Don't you remember?"

Vaguely it came back to her—the little people, their flower houses, and the quest. She awoke more fully, but her body felt heavy, sluggish, too tired to move. "I know the quest is important," she murmured, "but I'm so sleepy. I can't move yet…" Her eyes closed, and images of the beautiful horse, her parents and Sasha streamed in a moving picture before her eyes. It felt so real, like she was actually with her parents, the three of them so happy together. If only she could spend a little more time with them, Katie knew she could convince them not to get divorced.

"Thank the guardians that their magic doesn't seem to work as well on me," muttered Za, continuing to drag her.

"Where are you going?" warbled a sweet voice.

Katie looked up. Allura stood next to her, waving her gauzy wings. Hard to tell exactly what color they were, even though they were see-through, there were bits of sparkling color throughout.

"It's time for us to leave," Za said gruffly.

"You may leave," sang Allura, "but if you take your friend like this, she will lose her free will forever."

"And I suppose that has a meaning?" Za asked sarcastically.

"She is safe here," continued Allura.

Katie closed her eyes again, feeling like she was in a protective cocoon. *Nothing to worry about. Only the peace of these sweet dreams. Or were they real?* But Za and Allura's conversation was too distracting for her to fall back into dreams.

"She'll never get home," protested Za.

"Home," chirped Allura merrily. "Who is to say where her true home is? Perhaps it is here, with us."

I wonder if it is. Katie thought groggily.

Za snorted. "You're not going to get me to believe that."

"Ahh, but, unlike yourself, this one is a kindred spirit. We find it easy to share visions with her. Perhaps the Song Seed sent her to help us with our creation dreaming?"

"Ridiculous!" shouted Za. Katie could hear the fluttering sound of the other fairies hovering around her. "Katie wants to go home. You have to free her from this spell."

Yes, home. I want to go home. Katie forced her eyes open.

"It is no spell," Allura calmly hummed. She looked down at Katie. "It's your choice. Don't you want to stay with your parents and finish the movie?"

Katie nodded. *I want to stay with my parents.*

Allura sang softly, and Katie felt the soft tug of sleep, of dreams, of sweet oblivion, pulling her back down, down into sweet darkness, into rest. Still she willed her eyes to remain open.

"Only through her own desire, and the will you would rob her of, can your friend return," said Allura. She pointed at Za. "And you are disturbing our peace, something we never allow." She looked at him sternly. "Be gone, or the madness will come upon you, and you will no longer know yourself or anything else."

Before she sank back into dreams, Katie caught a quick glimpse of the hopeless look Za gave her before he walked out of the flower village… alone.

CHAPTER SEVENTEEN

The Lion's Wishes

The gong rang, and the fairies came to take Katie outside, as they had done for a dozen nights. Katie sat in a circle with them under the stars and feasted. Then Allura beat the drum, dum-dum-dee-dum. The yellow fairy played sweet notes on a flute, and someone strummed a harp. Katie hummed Mom's song and the fairies took up the refrain instantly, whirling and twirling in a fluttering dance as they flittered off the ground and waltzed in the air. *If only Mom could see this!*

There was only a quarter moon left in the sky. *That matters,* remembered Katie, but she couldn't remember why. Katie smoothed her braid, forgetting the uneasy thought, and joined the joyful dancers, leaping in her best arc, pirouetting around in a circle, wishing she had wings so that she could dance as the fairies did.

The evening wore on, and Katie wasn't sure if she lay in her flower house dreaming, or if she was really here, spinning under the stars with the fairies. They sang to the song weave within the soil. She watched fairies flit into the air and connect gossamer strands with the starry light in the stars, forming into gorgeous designs, like millions of unique and individual snowflakes sewn together, bringing beauty, vibrancy, and thriving life back down to the earth. She was tired when the first streaks of dawn lit the sky with peach and gold and Katie walked with the other fairies back to the flower houses, lying gratefully on her comfortable bed.

Reality blurred straight into dream, and Katie continued to dance with the fairies, only this time she had wings, this time she flew a graceful ballet in the air. Katie snuggled down into satiny petals.

Warm. Cozy. She curled against something soft, purring. "Sasha! You're here!"

"Of course," replied the cat, calmly licking her fur.

"You can talk!" exclaimed Katie, surprised the cat was speaking to her out loud and not just in her mind.

The cat sniffed. "*All* cats can talk."

"I mean, I can understand you," Katie corrected herself.

"You've always understood me well enough," replied the cat. "Could you pet that spot on my chest? You know, the one I really like."

Katie found the soft spot and rubbed it gently with her forefinger.

"Mmmmrrrmmmrrr," purred the cat.

"Oh, Sasha, I missed you so much. I'm so glad you're back."

The cat stood up and stretched. "Let's go outside, climb a tree, look around."

"Okay," answered Katie, opening her eyes. She stared up at the billowing petal ceiling. Sasha wasn't there anymore. Her stomach knotted into a hard ball. *Must have been another dream.*

Bright noon sun filtered through the fabric, making the whole room glow rose pink. It seemed strange to be awake during the day: the fairies always did their feasting and dancing at night, and slept during the day. Katie wiggled her feet outside the shelter, feeling the sun warm on her toes. They brushed against something furry and breathing. *Sasha? Maybe it wasn't a dream*. Katie eagerly crawled out of the room.

She knelt on all fours, gasping. "Kira? How did you get here? Did Dania send you?" she asked, wrapping her arms around the beautiful animal.

Kira stood up and walked slowly, turning her head back towards Katie.

"You want me to follow you?" asked Katie, wondering if this too was a dream. She bit her lip hard to find out. Ouch! *But the dreams were so real. Maybe that would hurt, even in a dream*?

Kira continued walking towards the meadow.

Might as well follow. Even if it is another dream, it ought to be a sweet one. But if it wasn't a dream, she ought to say goodbye to the fairies. They'd been so lovely to her. "Just a minute," Katie told the lion, looking around at the odd-shaped houses and trying to figure out which one belonged to Allura.

As if tuned to her wishes, Allura stepped out of a lavender flower house, blinking against the bright sun. "Have you decided to leave us?"

"I-I'm not sure," stammered Katie, "Am I awake?"

The notes of Allura's sweet laugh lingered the air. "Oh, you are awake. As awake as anyone in this life of illusion." And then, she sang a song that sounded both well-known and strange, coming, as it did, from a fairy. "Row, row, row your boat, gently down the stream. Merrily, merrily, merrily, merrily. Life is but a dream."

The other fairies stumbled sleepily out of their homes. "Does our guest leave us?" asked the blue fairy.

"I don't want her to go!" cried the smallest fairy.

Allura pointed at Kira. "A tree spirit's familiar is here."

Seidon suggested Dania might be a tree spirit, mused Katie. "What's a familiar?" she asked.

"Why, it's a creature whose perspective one takes. One can look through the creature's eyes, see the world from her point of view, so to speak," replied Allura. "Odd that *you* don't know that, considering your talents..."

"Why would a tree spirit send her familiar?" asked the green fairy, flapping her wings in front of Allura's face.

"I don't know," answered Allura, leaning her head to one side to get away from the flapping wings and staring straight at Katie. "I hope you don't leave us. It is a joy to create with you."

"Create?" asked Katie, confused. "All I've done is dream."

"Ahh, but dreams are the first step to any creation," sang Allura.

"Be careful, you might sprout wings," giggled the green fairy.

"Oh, don't let her go!" sobbed the smallest fairy.

"Shhh!" hushed the blue fairy. "You know we never keep folk against their will."

The pretty yellow fairy looked straight at Katie. "Is it really your will to leave us? To leave the bursting, vital joy of life? To leave the dancing, leaping, spiraling spinning wonder of it all? Why, you haven't even seen our seeding ceremonies."

Katie rubbed sleep from her eyes. *Doesn't feel natural to be awake during the day anymore.* "I'd like to stay," she murmured, then glanced at Kira. "But..."

Allura tilted her head, making her red, gold, orange, yellow, flaming sunrise hair stream behind her. "It's your decision, of course, but be sure. Once you leave, it's hard to find us again."

Kira took a step away from the flower village, distracting her from Allura's words. *The lion wouldn't be here without good reason.* "It's been lovely here with all of you," said Katie, "but I think I'd better go. Dania said the Goddess might have plans for me," she added, feeling more alert now that her mind was made up. "Where's Za?" asked Katie. "I can't go without him."

"He went his way long ago," cheeped Allura. "Nothing to fear. If it is meant, your threads will weave you back together."

Katie frowned. A dim image of Za giving her a sad look flickered at the back of her mind. "Which way did he go?"

But the fairies didn't answer. Instead, they immersed Katie in song, telling her of the warmth of sun, the sweetness of water, the brightness of life. The fairies surrounded her with lightly beating wings, guiding her gently back to the flower houses. Katie struggled against the temptation to rest again in their sweet dreams. Instead she walked down the grassy path and into the meadow where Kira waited. With every step she felt steadier and more wide awake. The dreamy haze that clouded her vision cleared, but not all the way. It was like the visions she'd had with the fairies superimposed upon her waking life, so that now she could see patterns in all the dreams, waking and sleeping, connecting the way the plants grew up from the soil with the sounds of music, so one green shoot hummed a middle C and another throaty pitcher plant sang a low G. All at once, she understood the way the fairies singing had guided the growth of the plants. Even the meadow looked entirely different. The colors were so incredibly bright and there were so many shades of green: emerald, avocado, lime, jade, olive, pea green and sea green. Why hadn't she noticed there were so many shades before? And the air was full of sparkles, as if it were alive and dancing.

Katie stood next to Kira. "I don't have Za, or my back-pack, or the fairies anymore," she said, "but at least I have you, Kira. You'll help me find the Winged Ones, won't you?"

Of course Kira didn't answer. *I wish Za's guardian had given me a charm so I could talk to Kira.*

"I'm sure going to hate leaving this place. Those fairies are something, aren't they Kira?" she asked, turning around for one last look at the flower village. She gasped. Where the fairy village had been was nothing but the green meadow. The large flower houses had shrunk to the size of normal flowers: daffodils, roses and tulips. Not even a hint remained of the fairies or their homes. "They're gone!" cried Katie.

After a moment of stunned silence, Katie said, "You'll have to show me which way to go, Kira." Katie turned back around.

Kira was not there.

CHAPTER EIGHTEEN

Katie's Choice

"Kira!" shouted Katie. She waited a moment, straining her ears to hear Kira's roar. Then she shouted even louder. "Kira! Kira!"

Katie shielded her eyes with her hand, blocking out the bright sun, squinting to see the lion. She bent down, examining the fragile meadow grass. There should be some sign of Kira: flattened grass, or a track beside the creek. She could follow that.

Katie walked carefully back and forth, keeping an eye out for large shimmering flowers so she wouldn't fall through a gate. She turned around in circles, checking every inch around the spot where she'd seen Kira waiting for her.

No sign. No sign of Kira at all. Almost like the lion had vanished—or never been there, just like those fairy dreams. "Kira!" Katie shouted again, even though her throat was growing hoarse.

There was no answer. Katie's shoulders slumped. Tears ran down her cheeks. She'd never get home now. She didn't even know where she was.

Katie searched the sky, hoping for a glimpse of fairies. She raced back to where the fairy village had been, veering just in time to avoid a sudden, shimmering and lurid green bloom.

"My bloom," a quiet, almost imperceptible voice whispered. Katie shivered. It was that voice again. "Allura!" called Katie. But she couldn't see anyone around. She was completely alone.

The meadow remained peacefully, tranquilly, horribly silent. She didn't know which way to go. If she kept running, she might stumble into one of those wavering, heat-mirage sort of gates. Katie threw herself to the ground and curled into a little ball. *I wish I was home.* She shut her eyes tight; hoping that when she opened them this whole adventure would vanish like a nightmare.

Katie took slow, deep breaths, trying to quell the sick feeling in her stomach, to slow her thump-thump-thumping heart. Somehow being on a strange world hadn't been quite so terrifying when she'd had a companion, even one like Za.

In and out, she breathed, counting each breath the way Mom had taught her to do when she was upset, so that she wouldn't have room for worries. In one, out two, in three.

Katie's pulse slowed. Her head felt light, seemed to expand, like a helium balloon. Colors wove themselves in patterns before her closed eyes. She watched, fascinated, until she felt herself spinning into an intricate web.

A voice broke her reverie, "We are each a strand in the weaving. We weave with the very threads we are woven of," said a soothing voice.

Katie cautiously opened her eyes. Standing before her was a silver-grey mare with wings sprouting from her sides. Both the mane and the wings had a pale blue, yellow, violet and green sheen. Katie stared, awed. At last, she found her voice. "Are you one of the Winged Ones?"

The horse thrust her nose up and down and whinnied. Then Katie heard that same comforting voice in her mind. "I am *your* Winged One."

Katie opened her eyes wide. *Was she still having fairy dreams?*

"I am really here," the horse spoke again in her mind. "I have always been with you."

Katie sat up, wiping the grass off her pants. "I've been searching everywhere for the Winged Ones. Why couldn't I find you?"

"You weren't paying attention. You did not embrace your quest. You were asleep!" the shiny silver horse explained. "Now, with the help of the lion, you have chosen to awaken."

Katie rubbed the horse charm on her wrist. No wonder she hadn't noticed the wings, they were carved flat against the horse's body. The horse knelt down, camel-like, so that Katie could mount. "Come."

Katie walked closer. The mare nuzzled her hand. Thrilled at the touch, Katie climbed up. Joy bubbled in her heart as she sat on the winged horse.

"Are you ready?" asked the horse.

Ready was too simple a word for the emotion Katie felt. She was ecstatic! She felt like dancing on clouds, flying in the sky, skipping on a rainbow.

The horse lifted effortlessly into the air. This smooth soaring felt nothing like the heavy flight of the dragon. Holding onto the glittering mane, Katie gripped tightly with her thighs, feeling one with the animal. "How can you speak in my mind and read my thoughts?"

The horse snorted. "That is your gift, not mine. You have been too busy and disbelieving in yourself to understand it before."

"What is your name?" Katie thought.

"Wind," came the returning thought. "Wind is everywhere and nowhere. Wind carries messages on the air, the elemental you humans can't live without for even a few minutes. Wind travels lightly, sees everything, including the song weave throughout the earth. Wind is my essence, my nature, my source of flight." The horse whinnied. "Change comes on the wind." Wind turned her head, making her mane of sparkling hair fly. "Now, you must decide whether or not you wish me to take you back through the winds of time and space to your world."

"Of course I want to go home!"

The horse curved into a glide. "First I must show you something." Wind turned completely, flying in the other direction with dizzying speed. The fairy meadow streaked by in a blur, and then the blue of the lake.

"Where are we going?" asked Katie.

Wind didn't reply. Her wings flapped hard, lifting them over the golden mountains. Katie looked down at the place of boulders where she'd met the scorpion, and then they were above the marsh. Wind circled for a few minutes. "Hold on tight," the horse directed telepathically. "I will take you as close as I can."

Thick fog swirled around them. Katie shivered. Wind's wings beat faster and faster, like a fan, and suddenly a tunnel opened up in the fog, leading straight down from them to the marsh below.

Za lay, as if unconscious, beside heaps of bleached white driftwood. "Za!"

"He can't hear you," said Wind. "All he can hear are words from the Poison One. Once they sneak inside those thoughts take over a person's mind."

Katie clutched Wind's silky mane. This was the first time someone had mentioned the Poison One without her feeling the internal watcher. Somehow being with Wind made Katie feel safe and protected, even from whatever it was that lay in wait within her own mind. She peered through the clearing in the fog, trying to see the Poison One. "What is it? All I see is Za and driftwood."

Wind flicked her ears. "I do not know what form the Poison One has chosen in this time and place. I can't get close enough to see, but notice how the strands in the song weave shrivel and die in this area?"

Katie looked down, and with Wind's help she could see a beautiful web of light running through the ground. The interconnected snowflake patterns of light abruptly ended in dead curled and shrunken ends several yards before Za. "When the song threads wither, life dies," explained Wind. "If you leave now, Za will die."

Poor Za! What was he doing back in the swamp? Fear and anger mixed with Katie's concern. She didn't want to go down there. She didn't. Katie groaned. *If only Za hadn't deserted me, he'd be fine and we could both go home.* A surge of sudden heat flushed all over Katie's body. Za looked so puny now, so insignificant. *Why had he been so stupid? He should never have left her.* A film swam before her eyes, so that Katie could hardly see. *What did she care about Za anyway? He was annoying, arrogant, and just plain weird looking. She wasn't going down there. Wind didn't even know what the Poison One was, but clearly it had gotten Za. It would get her too! Za had made his choices. He'd just have to live with them. Even if it meant his life ended here, with the Poison One, whatever it was.*

Wind jolted and they took a dive. A dreadful shudder moved the horse's flank, and then she righted herself, flying back up towards the sky, away from the fog that quickly closed in again, blocking Za from view.

The oily film that hung before Katie's eyes lifted. Her body cooled. "Wh-what happened?"

"That was a dangerous thing to do," scolded Wind. "Always think truth near the Poison One, or you are doomed. It feeds on lies."

Katie tightened her thighs around the mare's back. "What are you talking about?"

Wind's thought continued with a note of disapproval in Katie's mind. "When you lied to yourself about Za deserting you, you opened the door to the Poison One."

"That wasn't a lie!" exclaimed Katie. "He *did* leave me alone with the fairies."

Wind tossed her head, making her mane fly.

In her mind, Katie saw the devastated expression on Za's face when she wouldn't get up and the fairies forced him to leave her.

Katie's questions burst forth in a rush. "I don't understand what Za is doing here. Why didn't his journey song tell him the way? Didn't he see his Winged One?"

Wind's answer played like a movie in her mind: Za wandering in the meadow, his strange-looking Winged One (whatever it was, it certainly wasn't a horse) right beside him, and Za passing by without noticing it. And then she felt like she, herself, was Za, walking despondently across the meadow. She felt Za's shame at having left her, knowing the quest was something the two of them were supposed to do together. She felt Za's worry and concern for her, lost in fairy dreams. She felt Za's fear, burning his strange, alien nerves, when he considered the risk of returning and losing himself in fairy madness. Then she felt Za's resolve to find Kira, to send Kira back to rescue Katie. Katie tried to close her mind against Za's depression as he desperately searched for Kira, but it smothered her like an avalanche. She merged with his hopelessness and despair as he blindly trudged. And then, at last, the joy of finding Kira by the lake, of gesturing and signing until Kira understood, so that the lion followed Za back to the fairy meadow. Katie watched the lion lope ahead of Za towards the flower village. Za ran fast, trying to keep up, eager to see her again, to make sure she was unharmed. He saw the shimmering crimson flower too late. The gate sucked him in, spinning him down into a vortex. Katie felt his sick panic as he fell screaming into the hole.

"I'm sorry about Za," Katie's voice choked up. *Poor, poor Za.* In a way, she knew how it felt to be Za, now. She'd felt his feelings. Katie swallowed hard. He'd found Kira, sent her back. He hadn't deserted her, and he would have seen the flower gate in time if he hadn't been so worried about her. How could she abandon him to the Poison One? He'd die, and it'd be her fault. Katie gripped Wind's mane firmly. "What do you expect me to do?" she whispered. "If I go near the P-p…you know, it will get me too!"

Wind swooped down, hovering just above the fog bank. "You may halt the Poison One and close the fuming gate. Your gift will give you a chance."

"If my gift really is this ability to communicate with all sorts of animals and even elementals, like the water in the lake, then I'll have to speak with the…the…" The last two words came out in a whisper. Katie clenched her teeth. The whole situation was awful. She didn't want to go. But Za was trapped, and she was the only one who could save him from what Amy would call *a fate worse than death.* Katie buried her face in Wind's mane. 'I'll go."

"You must hurry!" Wind mind-spoke. "There's only a sliver of moon left. After the third moon wanes, we will lose our time to pass safely back to your world."

CHAPTER NINETEEN

Poison

The horse dove straight down so that Katie's ears popped. She held on tight, her arms wrapped around Wind's neck as the horse landed with a soft thud.

Katie blinked. Damp gray fingers of fog wrapped themselves around her. "What do we do next, Wind?"

Wind's whole body quivered. "I can't stay here." Wind picked one of her hooves up out of the mud. "You'll have to do the rest on your own."

"What!" Katie cried. "You can't leave me!"

"I have to," replied Wind. "The only way to get near the Poison One is to share a common bond with it. I have no such resonance."

"Well, then I won't be able to get near it either," declared Katie. "You might as well just fly me back up now. I don't have anything in common with it."

"Ah, but you do," replied Wind.

Katie broke into a sweat despite the icy air. Wind spoke with such absolute conviction that Katie knew she must really have something in common with the Poison One, but what could it possibly be? And how could she even find the Poison One in all this fog? She didn't even know what it looked like! "I don't know which way to go. I'm scared."

"Follow your fear and it will lead you to the Poison One," said Wind. "But be careful. Once you find it, the Poison One will find your worst fault."

My worst fault. Katie quaked in the clammy fog and her teeth clack-clacked with fear. *Wanting my own way too much? Losing my temper? What is it?*

Wind's ears pricked up. "Before I go, take a hair from my mane. Perhaps it will help you."

One long moon-colored strand of hair slipped into Katie's palm. "Wait," said Katie. "I'm not sure I can do this alone."

"Alone is the only way you can do it." The mare knelt down and gently tilted Katie off her back onto a clump of marsh grass. "Good luck, human child," mind-whispered Wind as she flew back into the sky. Katie was left with nothing but the hair from Wind's mane. It glittered hidden color, like an opal. Wrapping the coarse hair around and around her wrist, Katie tied it into a bracelet.

Her legs felt watery as she tried to stand. Cold fog completely engulfed her. In the distance, she heard a faint, mocking laugh. Goose bumps raised on the backs of her legs. She instinctively turned to go the other direction, away from that awful laugh, and then she remembered: *follow your fear*. The laughter howled gleefully, and Katie forced herself to take one step after another in its direction. "Bring her to me!" commanded the evil voice Katie recognized all too well. Instantly, ghostly fog-men took form in the mist, surrounding her with their swaying figures and herding her towards the sniggering laugh. It was the direction she needed to go anyway, so Katie didn't try to repel the damp hands pushing against her back. The ground crunched underfoot. She bent down to look at the smooth ivory rocks and driftwood. Not driftwood at all. *Skulls. And bones. Mounds of them heaped one on top of another.* One huge rib cage reminded her of dinosaur bones. It still had a bit of iridescent green scale. Perhaps this was what had happened to the baby dragon's mother. And there, next to it, was the skeleton of a lion. The furry tail was still attached. *Oh, no! Not Kira.* The bitter taste of bile filled her mouth.

Her heart sank, but she made herself stand back up, look away, and continue to move forward. The rotting stench of carcasses filled Katie's nostrils. Patches of cold gray fog interspersed with sultry heat. It grew hotter and hotter and the fog thickened so that she could hardly see when she rounded a bend and faced a huge tarry pool. It pulsed hypnotically and she couldn't take her eyes off of the bubbling tar-pit. Where was the Poison One? *What* was the Poison One?

The fog-men pressed her closer to the pool before dispersing back into undefined whorls of gray. The mist lifted a bit and she saw a body lying beside the tar-pit. "Za!"

He didn't move. He looked so pale, almost white, not his usual glowing amethyst. "Za! Can you hear me?"

A horribly recognizable voice rolled off of the pool, whispering inside and outside of her head. "You've finally come." The liquid rippled. The voice in her head fizzled and buzzed. Still, she somehow knew exactly what it was saying. "I've been waiting for you." *Could the Poison One* be *this tar-pit?*

"What have you done to Za?"

"Stay and help me," garbled the pool, flat and glistening.

"Never!"

The pool frothed. "I have the power!" It bubbled up and Katie's head filled with a burring noise. Still, there was no mistaking the pool's meaning. "You *will* obey me!"

"Why would I?" Katie checked Za's pulse. *Weak and erratic.*

"It is I who opened the fuming gate linking our worlds." The pool beat out a mesmerizing tempo and Katie felt her whole body pulsing in time. "It is I who made the troubles in your family," it boasted. "It is I who brought you here."

"You?" she whispered, feeling feverish. *It must have been watching me for some time now, even at home.* She forced herself to look away from the pool and to focus on Za, shaking him. "Wake up, Za, wake up!"

The pool gurgled. "Ha! You think this feeble one will help you? It took a while, but I found his flaw: his fatal arrogance. The arrogance the young Stellan uses to hide his insecurity, the feeling of not being enough and so he pretends to be more than he is."

Katie's throat constricted. Arrogance really was Za's flaw. If the Poison One found Za's fault, it would find hers. She continued to shake Za, but his body rolled back and forth, limp, almost lifeless.

The pool's slick voice said, "He is already burned out. Soon, I will consume the rest of his life force." The pool splashed. "My power grows with every being I devour."

Katie stroked Za's pale face. "Please wake up, Za."

"He's mine," said the Poison One, forming a face on the flat surface. It added conversationally, "I've taken his will. Of course, I was careful to make it seem like his own desire, his own choice, as I always am when I tempt people to serve me," the pool bragged. "Still, a few Ashans have discovered my methods and now I'm forced to hide out on this backwater world."

Asha. She'd heard that name before. *Wasn't that Za's Mother's world*?

"Now that I've found you," the pool gushed happily, "I will soon be strong enough to return to Earth. With your help, I will be able to go deeper into the minds of humans. They will all do my bidding."

"You're evil!" Katie tried not to focus on the voice, but it seeped into her skull, impossible to tune out.

The Poison One spouted, "Together, we will spread the fear of survival, until everyone believes there is not enough. This idea of scarcity will pit people against each other and nature, separating all. Differences will be reasons to feel superior and some people will use that as a justification to dominate others, forcing whole groups into slavery."

"We've already had that," snapped Katie. "We fought the Civil War to end slavery." Katie remembered how proud her dad had been of his Mexican heritage when he told her how Black people escaping slavery from the United States were granted safe asylum in Mexico.

"It's not so easy to defeat me," gloated the tar-pit, boiling and bubbling higher and higher, sniggering and snickering, and then chanting hysterically, "I shame. I blame. I criticize." Little geyser spouts spun in tempo to the words. "I consume. I burn out. I gobble." It grew larger and larger until Katie could see a tarry shape forming in the center of the pit. "I devour. I take. I want. I want it all!" The tarry geyser gathered itself together into one gigantic spinning vortex. "I WANT it all! I must grow bigger and bigger and bigger," it surged up higher, spinning so fast that watching made Katie feel like she was spinning too. "There's not enough for others!"

"That's not true!" Katie shouted. "Dad's growing a forest garden to bring back nature's abundance for *everyone*, including the wildlife!"

The tar-geyser's belly expanded and it jetted streams of sticky goop and jeered, "He's a loser! He can't even support his own family."

Katie glared and repeated the words Dad said so often, "He's trying to change the system!"

"My system," The Poison One said confidently, spinning a little more slowly. "My system is nearly everywhere on Earth. Your father will never break free. He can't do it alone! No one can."

Katie's heart sank. *That's what Mom had said.* Tearing her eyes away from the spouting tar, Katie reminded herself that changing the system wasn't her problem. All she needed to do was get Za up so they could leave. She felt the faint throb of his pulse. *Still alive.* His fingers clutched the pebble. If only it really were a magic pebble.

"Join me and you will have all the magic you need." The Poison One changed its bragging tone to a seductive whisper. It flattened back into a still calm lake.

"I don't believe you," whispered Katie, but it was becoming harder and harder to distinguish her own thoughts from those of the silky voice inside and outside her head. She forced herself to focus on Za. He was so thin. "Wake up! Please wake up," said Katie, looking for something to help him. Her eyes swept the desolate land. The only beauty came from Wind's bracelet. Katie quickly slipped it off and tied it onto Za's bony wrist.

As soon as she took the bracelet off her wrist, the static vanished and the Poison One's voice broadcast crystal clear, like a radio station that was tuned all the way in. "Come to me," it said invitingly. Katie lifted Za's shoulders and propped him up into a sitting position, leaning him against a pile of bleached out old bones. He weighed so little.

A cloud floated off the pool and followed Katie. It wrapped around her shoulders, moved sinuously across her face, caressed her cheek, feeling pleasant and warm. "Touch me," the pool cooed, and she felt tempted, trying to remember why she couldn't trust it. *It would feel so wonderful to be warm and comfortable again*. The part of her that screamed, '*Danger!*' receded deep down, a faint echo. She could no longer tell her own thoughts from those of the smooth voice, which seeped inside her bones, flowed in her blood, and crooned, "I'll take you back through the gate. I'll take you home. You'd like that, wouldn't you? Home?"

Katie clutched that one word as if it were a life raft in this foggy sea. "Home. Yes, home," Katie repeated. Home was where she wanted to go. She knew that. Katie let go of Za and staggered hypnotically towards the pool. "Home."

CHAPTER TWENTY

The Shadow Voice

"Yes, home," repeated the pool, and the glistening lake surface glinted invitingly. "Touch me, and your troubles are over," it promised.

An overwhelming desire to put her hand out and stroke the velvety softness, the sleek blanket of liquid, filled Katie. She kept her hand stiffly by her side. "Aren't you poison?" she asked, trying to remember.

"I'm not poison," reassured the pool. "I'm nice and soft and I can help you."

Yes, help. Katie moved a step closer to the satiny midnight pool.

"Katie!" An urgent voice called her from behind.

Katie tore her eyes away from the pool and glanced back. "Za, you're awake!"

Za struggled to sit up on the pile of bones. His eyes looked huge in his hollow starved face.

"Are you alright?" Katie asked slowly, still feeling the drumming tug of the pool and hearing the trance-inducing voice in her ear, "Touch me, touch me..." The words beat in rhythm with her heart so that all she wanted to do was to move closer to the pool, to feel its warm surface.

Za grimaced. "Something...brought...me back."

Katie pointed vaguely at his wrist. "The hair."

"Look at me," crooned the pool. "Come to me now, and I'll even get your parents back together."

I'd give anything to have my parents back together—happy—the way we used to be. Dad and Mom laughing all the time. Mom singing. Katie turned back to the pool.

"I can fix everything," the pool continued enticingly. "I'll even make your parents forget the awful things you said."

Yes, they'll forgive me, then. She moved towards the shining water. She stood poised on the edge, ready to step in.

"No!" shouted Za.

Katie hesitated.

She could hear Za's footsteps rattling the pile of bones. He clutched her arm weakly and led her a few paces away from the pool. "Don't touch it," he said urgently. "That's... how it got me." Za paused, seeming to gather strength into his gaunt haggard body. "There's a way...to resist."

Katie blinked, trying to clear her vision, trying to think. "Resist?" Katie said, squinting at Za past the haze that clouded her eyes. *Why would I want to resist the warm velvet pool?*

Feathery spray kissed Katie's cheek. "Come, touch me. I have what you need."

The pool can do what it says. Katie turned back to face it.

Za slapped Katie's face.

Katie rubbed her stinging cheek. "Why'd you do *that?!?*"

"Listen!" Za said. "Listen to my words and watch the pool!" His body wobbled with the effort it took to stay upright. He planted his big purple feet firmly on the ground, digging in his long toes and staring intently into Katie's eyes. "Grateful...you're here."

The pool's seductive voice hummed, "He lies. He's never grateful about anything."

That's true, thought Katie, but then she remembered Za thanking Kira after the scorpion. She half-turned back to him. He was a pale, washed out lavender in the evening light. His knees buckled as he crumpled back to the ground, which was littered with feathers, scraps of fur, red splashes of blood and, of course, the bones. "I am glad you came with me…on this quest," said Za.

The pool glurped. "He's just trying to get something out of you with flattery."

Katie gave Za a suspicious look. "Why are you saying all this *now*?"

"It's true!" answered Za, his tired voice ringing with conviction. "You helped with the dragon…the scorpion…the fish-man. I never would've survived…without you."

"Za's right," said Katie, and, as she spoke, she saw the edges of the pool shrivel inward.

"One thing I like…about you," continued Za, forming each word with obvious exhausted effort, "is that you're brave. Brave as any Stellan."

A little streak of gladness shot through Katie's heart. "I *was* brave," she murmured.

The pool squealed. "What use is bravery when you never think of anyone but yourself?" it taunted. "You're selfish! Your parents must be glad to be rid of you. You're the reason they want a divorce!"

"No!" cried Katie, but she felt doubt. She had said such awful words.

"You called them liars!" Heat rolled off the pool. "Said you wished they weren't your parents. Said you hated them!"

"I didn't mean it!" cried Katie but the words she could never forget, never take back, were stuck in Katie's mind and she recalled herself screaming "I hate you! I hate you! I hate you!"

"That's right," the Poison One urged. Its center gushed upwards into a boiling geyser with hollow eyes at the center and a huge mouth spouting globs of thick tar. "Remember it all. Remember how awful you are. Shame on you!"

Katie couldn't stop the memories. In her mind's eye, she saw once again how Mom's face had blanched white. She'd looked so stricken. Tears rolled down her cheeks. Dad frowned. "You don't mean this, Rosa."

Instead of apologizing, Katie threw her brush right at Mom. The hard bristles hit Mom and Katie saw blood dripping down Mom's cheek before slamming her bedroom door right in Dad's face and turning the lock.

She heard Mom sobbing and Dad soothing her, his footsteps heading to the bathroom down the hall and returning, probably with the first aide. She strained her ears, listening as Dad tried to comfort Mom, "Don't worry, Susan, she's still a child."

"Sh-she hates me." Mom sobbed even louder.

"She doesn't hate you," Dad murmured. "She has a temper but she will grow up and learn to control it. Things will be okay again, somehow. Even if we're not together, Katie will get through this."

Mom kept crying, but eventually her sobs quieted and then Dad had knocked on her door. Katie wouldn't open it. After trying for a long time, Dad said, "We'll talk later, Rosa," and she heard his footsteps fading away. Mom stayed a little longer begging her to open the door, but Katie couldn't face her.

"You see?" The gyrating tarry figure chortled. "You're not good enough. You're rude. Ungrateful. Selfish."

Katie collapsed to the ground, rolling into a hurt ball.

Za squeezed Katie's arm. "Don't listen!"

How could she not listen? What the tar-thing said was true.

The pool slurped and the tar-figure sank back into the flattened lake, only the hollows of its eyes still visible. Greasy waves lapped the bony shore, inches from Katie. "Come to me, and I will make it all better."

Za pressed the hair bracelet against Katie's forehead. "Don't give up Katie. Think of…the earth beneath our feet. Think of your own Earth. She loves all her creations, all of her expressions of life, and you are one of them. Earth loves you, Katie, just as you are and she wants you to come home."

"You're not on Earth," mocked the Poison One. "This little gnome cannot know how your planet feels about you or anything else."

"I feel the truth through the soles of my feet!" shouted Za.

"By now, even your Earth has forgotten all about you," continued the tar-thing in the rational voice it took along with the flat lake form. "Do you think she has time for such a trifling creature?"

True. Spray got in Katie's eyes, blurring her vision. *There was no way the Earth, with all her species of life, could care about her.*

"Exactly." The two eye sockets winked and smirked from the center of the pool. "Not only Earth but everyone else has forgotten you by now. Amy probably has a new best friend. And your parents must be relieved you're gone. Life will be simpler without a hot-tempered brat like you."

Katie gasped, feeling like she'd been punched in the stomach. *Life probably would be easier for her parents without her, especially now with the divorce. They wouldn't have to listen to her nonstop begging for a horse anymore.*

"Think of the Winged Ones," Za said, a new desperation in his voice.

Winged Ones? What were they? A vague image came into Katie's mind, but she didn't know what it was.

Za helped her to sit up, rocking her in his arms. "Don't give up, Katie!" He moved the hair bracelet around, stroking her head, her face, her neck, her arms, and her back. As he did, Katie felt tingles. The holy water Dania had made them drink fizzed inside her and some of the poisonous thoughts cleared so she could think again.

The pool spurted hot liquid around Katie, scalding her hand. "I want you!" spat the pool, flinging gobs of oily gook at her. "You!"

Katie stared at the boiling pool. *Why did I think I could swim in that?* It had tried to trick her. Kill her. She'd be just another pile of bones.

Suddenly her lethargy was replaced with white hot fury. Katie pitched a dirt clod into the pool. "Take that, you stinking cesspool!"

The pool gulped down the clod. *That could have been me.* Katie threw a rock into the pool. It sank with another gulp. "You're the one who should be ashamed, you evil greedy monster!" She threw a heap of dried out old bones into the pool, tossing in all her hurt, rage, guilt and shame along with the skeletons. Gulp. Gulp. Gulp. Sweat dripped down Katie's body in the raging heat. She grabbed the nearest thigh bone and heaved it in. "You hideous greasy pool!"

Shooting up into the enormous geyser, it stared at her from hollow eye cavities. The geyser grew bigger and bigger.

"I hate you!" shrieked Katie, continuing to throw everything she could get her hands on at the pool. "I hate you! I hate you! I hate you!"

The geyser loomed over Katie in a towering wave ready to crash down upon her head.

Za tugged frantically on her sleeve. "Not that way, Katie. Listen," he said frantically. "I like you because you're loyal. You've stuck with me during my journey quest."

Damp fog swirled around the broiling geyser.

"You're loyal, too," replied Katie slowly. "You found Kira and tried to come back for me."

Za's eyes lit with hope. "Turned out you're even a good storyteller." The tarry figure twisted and turned.

"Sometimes you're funny," said Katie slowly, watching the pool. *Was the geyser growing smaller?* Katie concentrated hard, trying to think of reasons she really liked Za, remembering Wind telling her to speak truth around the Poison One. "You have courage," said Katie slowly. *The tar-geyser* was *shrinking!*

"You've listened to me," added Za.

"You've listened to me, too," said Katie.

"No!" screamed the pool. *It was definitely shrinking!*

"I like you because you're my friend," continued Katie more confidently. "You saved me with your magic pebble."

Ear-splitting shrieks erupted from the shriveling pool.

Za never took his eyes off Katie. She had to strain her ears to hear him. "Friends…forever."

"Forever," agreed Katie, kneeling down. As she reached for his hand, the pool moaned again, "Noooo." The tar-figure was no longer visible, not even its eyes, and the pool receded fast, revealing mudflats.

Katie clasped Za's strange alien fingers, his long knuckles twining in her own. The hair bracelet around his wrist burst into a blazing rainbow of color. Katie watched, amazed, as it lit up their joined hands in a halo which grew larger and larger until it enveloped the two of them in a brilliant glory of light.

The pool shrank into something that resembled an asphalt lump.

"My parents do want me!" Katie cried, staring at the blob. "I don't need you to make them forget what I said. I can tell them I'm sorry!" Tears of relief rolled down Katie's cheeks.

Katie wiped her eyes. The last of the fog evaporated, so that she could see the blue sky above and the golden mountains in the distance. "I think we did it."

Za jumped up and down on his big feet. "We won, Katie!"

"Thanks to you," said Katie. "How did you figure out how to fight it?"

"I was here for long enough to realize the Poison One couldn't stand a true friendship like ours—the kind that can accept each other exactly as we are."

"And ourselves too," added Katie, thinking how close the pool had come to convincing her not to accept herself.

Now the fuming gate will close, just like Wind said. Katie's shoulders relaxed and everything took on a rosy glow. "We can go home."

"Yes!" said Za, staring at the sky. And then he gasped, "Oh no!" and pointed.

Katie looked up. The third moon was gone.

CHAPTER TWENTY-ONE

The Fuming Gate

Katie's heart sank. "We'll be trapped on this planet forever."

"I've failed my journey quest," Za said sadly. "I'll never be initiated now."

"I'm sorry, Za." Katie said gently. She craned her neck back, searching the sky for Wind. There was no sign of the horse. She clenched her teeth in despair.

Za sat slumped over with his head in his hands, humming his journey song.

Katie blinked hard, holding back tears. She stared at the last bit of fog hovering over the spot where the pool had been. Whorls of mist parted, revealing a huge portal. Katie jumped to her feet. "Look!" she exclaimed. "That must be the fuming gate."

A strong gust of wind blew the last fog away. "There's my living room! And there's Sasha!" She ran towards the cat and home, stopping herself a second before she stepped past the gate. She looked back at Za. "Come on! Come with me!"

Za looked at his feet, as if they might have an answer. Finally he said, "The quest isn't finished."

"But it is over," Katie said sadly, "We've failed." She yanked Za's twisty arm. "Now you *have* to come with me. It's the only way we'll get out of here."

Za didn't budge. He sang the last lines in his journey song.

Together seen
Winged Ones are
Flying serene
Home, home star

"I still haven't seen the Winged Ones all together, so the quest can't be over." Za pointed. "Go now. The gate's closing."

The words of Za's journey song echoed in Katie's mind: *Together seen.* She darted a yearning glance at her cozy living room. *One step and I'm home.*

Katie turned her back on the gate. "I'm staying," she said, resigned.

A loud boom rent the air and the earth shook around Katie, throwing her to the ground. The gate slammed shut.

ZA GAVE HER A HAND UP. "WHY DIDN'T YOU SAVE YOURself when you had the chance?"

"It is obvious you can't finish this quest by yourself," said Katie. "You need me."

Za curled his big toes deeper into the earth. "You've been a great help, Katie, but I really can finish on my own. All I need to do is see the Winged Ones all together."

"Your song doesn't mean that," Katie said. "Don't you see? It means *we* have to be together when we see the Winged Ones." She groaned. Something sharp jutted into her wrist.

Her charm bracelet snagged on a sharp bone. Katie untangled it. "You know, Za, we haven't met the tree yet."

Za's yellow eyes lit up. "Then you are right! The quest isn't over."

Katie scanned the desolate landscape. There wasn't a Winged One in sight. Nothing but mounds of bones, some with raw flesh still clinging to them. It was getting dark and they had no water, food, or blankets. Katie shivered. "If we can't find the Winged Ones, we'll never survive the night."

Za's long thumb rubbed against his brown jumpsuit. At least it didn't look any worse for wear. Not true for the two of them. Za's blue hair frizzed out in all directions and there wasn't a hint of white left on her torn T-shirt. "If we die, at least we'll have done something good with our lives."

Katie nodded soberly. "The Poison One will never hurt anyone again."

"We were a good team, weren't we?" said Za.

"Yeah," agreed Katie, watching healthy violet color stream back into Za's cheeks. He visibly filled with energy. Katie raised her eyebrows, puzzled.

"The pool was using my energy," Za answered her unspoken question. "I feel better now that we've contained it and when you gave me that bracelet, I somehow knew that I could suck energy in from the ground right through my feet." Za wiggled his toes.

Katie gave him a questioning look.

"Even here, where the earth has been so damaged and polluted, there is still health deep underneath. When I was trying to find the strength to bring you back, it felt like my feet grew roots and connected with the microbes in the soil." Za shrugged. "Like my soul met the soil and it helped me bring you back."

Katie gestured towards the pile of bones surrounding a little pool of clear water. "Was that here before?"

"No," said Za, and they both stared as green shoots rapidly grew. A frog croaked and jumped into the puddle. "The water is clearing!"

"I can see the song weave sewing itself back together," said Katie, pointing to the luminescent strands reconnecting and weaving closer to the area that had been the dead zone around the Poison One.

"Right," said Za, humming his journey song. The song lines wove together even faster, becoming once again part of a tapestry of interwoven beauty.

"I remember your guardian said the journey song would help harmonize us with this world's song weave. It must also help the song weave heal!" exclaimed Katie.

"Wow, we could stay here and repair the song weave."

Katie shook her head. "As amazing as it all is, I'm *not* spending the night here. Let's go."

"Wait!" said Za.

"No," replied Katie without stopping. "I can't stand another minute in this place, even if it is starting to miraculously heal."

"Look up!"

Katie craned her neck back. Two glowing objects drifted slowly towards them.

"Eek!" shouted Za.

"It's okay," Katie reassured. "Whatever they are, it doesn't look like they're harmful."

The bright spheres came closer and closer. Katie craned her neck.

Squinting, Katie tried to get a better look at the descending shapes. Maybe they were only light refracting on clouds?

Or? Katie almost didn't dare to hope. And then she saw two wings unfurl. "The Winged Ones!"

"Together seen, the quest assured," sang Za. Then he spoke, "We've seen them together. Now we *will* get home!"

Katie's eyes widened. "Za, I'm in your journey song! Your guardian knew all along that we'd do this quest together."

Za didn't answer. His gaze was riveted on the Winged Ones. Katie watched too as they landed with such agility that the heap of skulls barely moved. The Winged Ones glowed a pale yellow, so that the area around them lit up.

"Wind!" Katie put her arms around the horse's neck. "I didn't think you were coming back."

The horse nuzzled her hand and spoke in her mind, "In stopping the Poison One, you have accomplished more than you know."

"Is the Poison One gone forever?"

"We don't know yet," replied Wind. The mare's eyes widened and expanded, as if she were looking far beyond. "It's more a matter of it being in balance where it belongs, and not greedily expanding out of control."

Katie rested her weak exhausted body against the mare. "What are we going to do now, Wind?"

"I'll help you survive on this world," replied Wind. "In fifty of your Earth years, the moons will once again be three in the sky and I will be able to take you home then."

Fifty years! By then my parents will be old and none of my friends will know me, and Sasha will be dead. Katie recoiled as the full reality hit her. This time she couldn't hold back the tears. She blubbered and bawled, crying so hard she could barely breathe, her sides heaving against the mare's warm body.

CHAPTER TWENTY-TWO

The Grandmother Tree

Katie couldn't stop crying. The idea of never ever getting home, and fifty years might as well be never ever, was so horrible. "Calm yourself, human child," soothed Wind's soft mind voice "If you want to return home so badly, there is one way."

Katie hiccupped. "How?"

"We can harness the power of the Poison One and take it with us. It will thrust us so far out into the stars that it won't matter that we missed the moons. However, if we make the slightest mistake, the Poison One will feed off of our energy instead. Then it will grow, and we will be annihilated, worse than dead, as if we'd never been. No one will even remember us."

Katie caressed Wind's cheek. "I want to go home," she whispered. "I want to go home, but how can I ask you to risk something worse than death?"

Wind nuzzled her hand. "It's a risk I'm willing to take for you. I trust you. If you follow my directions exactly, we will make it." Wind regarded her with serious but gentle brown eyes. "Listen carefully. First you must pick up what's left of the Poison One. Be careful not to touch it. It still has the power to infect. Take hairs from my mane and weave them together into a small cloth. Use this to pick it up."

Moving quickly, Katie wove a cloth as best she could from Wind's opalescent hairs. Then she walked over to the Poison One. It had shrunk to the size of a golf ball. Careful not to touch it, she picked it up and wrapped the sticky ball into the cloth and then carried the remnants of the Poison One back to Wind.

On her way, she passed Za, who was patting one of his Winged One's tentacles. It resembled a giant octopus with wings. "Isn't he a beauty?" asked Za.

Katie grinned, glad to see Za so happy.

"I had no idea what my Winged One would look like," Za added. "Everyone's is entirely different, but Eek is just the most gorgeous ever!"

"Eek?" asked Katie.

Za patted the creature affectionately. "We have a tradition on Stella; our Winged Ones are always named after the word we say first upon seeing them."

Katie smiled at the custom, happy for Za. Her smile grew even bigger as she watched Za pick his way over the suction cups on the creature's thick tentacles.

Za smiled back at her, flashing his blue teeth. "We did it, Katie! We're going home."

Straddling Wind, Katie was careful to keep the repugnant ball in its hair wrapping. She gripped the horse with her thighs and used her free hand to hold her mane.

As soon as she was settled, Wind flew quickly away from the bones. Katie looked down. There were masses and masses of decomposing skeletons. All sorts of shapes and sizes, all sorts of bodies who had been trapped and lost their lives. She clenched her teeth. *If it hadn't been for Za's discovery about the Poison One's fear of friendship, my bones would be part of that pile.*

Katie watched Eek's tentacles flapping madly as the lit-up octopus zoomed through the sky. Wind followed in the direction of the dawning light, so that Katie began to see the ground below whiz by in a fuzzy blur. It was full day by the time Wind finally slowed and hovered over Dania's forest. The air was fresh and delicious and Katie gulped it in. "Why did you bring me back here?"

"If my plan is to work, we'll need the support of the trees."

Katie wondered what help trees could offer, but she didn't say anything. *Wind knows what she's doing*, Katie told herself. *She'll get me home.*

The horse stopped in front of Dania's tree home. Katie jumped off the mare. A large lion lay in front of the entry. "Kira!" she exclaimed, throwing her free arm around the lion, sinking her face into thick fur. "I was so worried. I was sure the Poison One got you."

Kira licked Katie's face once with her sandpaper rough tongue.

Za climbed down his flying octopus and walked over to the lion. He stooped and cautiously patted Kira's head. "Thank you for all your help."

"Where's Dania?" asked Katie, ducking her head into the dwelling. Dania wasn't there. Katie dashed around the meadow. She even ran down to Dania's sacred hot springs, but there was no sign of the golden lady anywhere.

The tree overhead rustled in a sudden breeze. "Here...." the leaves whispered.

Katie craned her neck back, looking for Dania high in the branches of the largest tree. "Are you up there?"

The leaves crackled again. "I am...Grandmother tree."

"You're the tree?" asked Katie, puzzled. And then she realized: *This is what Seidon and the fairies meant when they kept saying Dania was a tree spirit. She changes shape.* Katie looked at the tree on her charm bracelet. *I'll keep this bracelet for the rest of my life, to remind me of Dania, Seidon, Allura, and Wind*, Katie vowed silently to herself before saying, "We did it, Dania! We stopped the Poison One."

Air whooshed between the trees. Shush, shush, shush. The bark creaked. "You have…done well."

"I have it here," said Katie, holding the carefully wrapped ball closer to the tree.

Huge tree limbs waved wildly as though in a storm. Katie pulled the wrapped ball away and set it carefully onto the ground a safe distance away. "That isssss better," said the tree in her slow voice.

"We're going to go home," said Katie. "Wind said the trees can help us."

"We…try."

"How?" asked Katie. "What can trees do?"

"My sap…runs too slow…for speech." Branches seemed to reach for the sky and the trunk expanded and contracted, almost like it was breathing.

"Is it possible for you to take your woman form so we can talk?" asked Katie. "I have so much to tell you!"

"Not…the time," the tree answered slowly. "Only… when…at least one moon is in the sky…but you can join me…in the tree. Sit…back against my trunk."

Katie nestled against the roots of the giant tree, feeling embraced by the trunk. The tree looked like the biggest oak she'd ever seen with pearly-white smooth bark, the color of moonlight. If only Mom and Dad could both see it! They'd love this tree, the way both of them were always telling her stories about how sacred oaks were to their Celtic ancestors, like churches or cathedrals. Mom practically cried when she told her how most of the old oaks in Ireland had been chopped down over the centuries. During the five hundred years of colonization by the English, the Irish weren't even allowed to own trees! The few remaining large oak and ash trees in Ireland were mostly found on English estates.

Dania's tree sure was enormous. Letting go of all her worries, fears and struggles to get home again, Katie relaxed against the tree. *Just for a moment.* Taking in long, slow deep breaths of the wonderful fresh air, Katie's pulse slowed, giving her the odd sense of settling into rhythm with the tree, so that she could almost feel the sap flowing in the trunk as if it were her own blood flowing in her veins.

"There you are," said Dania, glowing from within the heartwood as her ethereal form settled down next to Katie. "I knew you could do it!"

Katie marveled at the solid and yet also porous trunk enveloping her. When she glanced at her arm, she saw that it was visible as a sort of light within the wood. Moving her arm, she watched the light move within the body of the tree, perfectly illuminating the outline of her hand. "Am I really in the heart of this tree with you?"

"Not your physical body," replied Dania, "but your spirit body. This talent of yours will be important. We know that you and many others will be able to work with nature intelligences to restore the places that were harmed during the long reign of the Poison One."

"*Who* knows?" asked Katie, a bit daunted by the size of the task. "You said, 'we.'"

Dania's pure light permeating the inside of the tree flickered and changed: warm gold, soft white, winking pink, yellow, blue, violet and green. "Oh, the trees know. They are ancient wise beings, informed by the stars and planetary bodies, and they speak with each other through both the atmosphere and the soil. Without them and the other plants there wouldn't even be life on your world. You are the children of the green growing beings. You are loved by them, as a mother loves."

"Amazing!" said Katie. This was something she had to share with Dad.

"Let me show you." Dania motioned for Katie to follow as her light body dived down the trunk into the roots. Katie's spirit body whisked right behind Dania. She felt herself go into the beautiful oak roots, almost as deep as the tree was high. And then she entered the thin strands wrapped around and between the roots.

"Fungi," explained Dania.

"Like mushrooms?" Katie asked.

"The mushrooms we see above ground are only the fruiting bodies of the fungi," said Dania. "Most of the fungal bodies are underground." Her light sparkled through many strands, like threads, thinning down to the size of fine hairs.

Katie twinkled along behind, feeling herself as the fungi, caressing the roots, wrapped around them in a sensual embrace, and then going throughout the soil in all directions, seeking nutrients. As soon as one of her fungal threads found nourishment then her whole fungal self knew and more threads began to turn in that direction.

"Each fungi has many strands, but they act as one body," said Dania, turning back. "What one discovers, they all know."

As Katie followed Dania's light back up the fungi, towards the tree, she lingered near the roots, tasting sugary nectar. The tree was feeding her fungal self this life-giving juice! Dania's glimmering light traveled up into the roots. Katie reluctantly left the delicious sweetness behind. As soon as she was in the roots, Katie felt the fungi feeding her tree self. This time it was water, nitrogen, phosphorus and other minerals she couldn't name.

Dania and Katie flowed up the trunk along with the nutrients, into limbs, branches and twigs and right into the green leaves. Her leaves danced in the zephyr breeze, loving the sunlight and absorbing it like sponges soaking up water.

Simultaneously, Katie sensed her physical body still leaning against the trunk of the tree, breathing in and out, breathing together with the tree, inside and outside, both giving each other what they needed—oxygen for her and carbon dioxide for the tree. It was all a giant exchange! She was still aware of the water coming up from the roots and she knew how she, as a tree, turned this water, light and air into sweet, sweet food. Enough sweet nourishment that it overflowed back down into the roots to feed the hungry fungi.

"It's incredible how we all work together: human, tree, fungi," whispered Katie, awed, as her spirit body settled back down beside Dania in the heartwood.

"You humans really aren't so different from fungi, going out in all directions, seeking nourishment. Although as individuals, humans are separate in their bodies, Humanity itself may also function like a single being. When one of you learns something, the knowledge quickly spreads to others. This connectivity will allow you to support each other just like the fungi."

Katie listened. What Dania said reminded her of the song weave Wind had shown her in the earth, and how every line of song influenced the whole composition.

"What I'm saying is that as you heal yourselves you will also be healing your Earth," said Dania.

Maybe she knew what Dania meant. Katie could still see the image of green shoots growing around the small, clear pond after she and Za had healed their relationship and used their friendship to shrink the Poison One.

Dania continued, "Imagine how it will be when beautiful forests and green plants grow everywhere they'd naturally grow, the waters are clear, birds sing, and wildlife thrives."

Wind neighed. The mare's mind-voice penetrated the trunk. "Hurry, Katie. We have to go."

"It's time, Katie," said Dania. "Go with my blessing."

Katie choked up. "Thanks. I wish I could spend more time with you."

Dania smiled. "Listen to the trees and we will guide you wherever you are."

"Katie!" Wind's call reverberated within the trunk. "It's now or never."

Dania gave her a push and instantly Katie's energy body merged back together with her physical body, still sitting at the base of the trunk.

CHAPTER TWENTY THREE

Going Home

Za helped Katie up. "I guess this is it."

Katie flung her arms around him in a hug. Za's skin went from purple to pink, and he smiled shyly as he stepped out of her embrace. "Eek says we have to go first so that we can feel the full thrust of energy from the ball when you use it." He stopped speaking and fidgeted from foot to foot. "I just want you to know that I wasn't making it up with the Poison One. I really do consider you a friend, one of the best."

Katie's throat constricted. *This is the last time I'll ever see Za.* She took his hand in hers. "It's been great getting to know you." Her voice choked up. "I mean, really great." The words were so inadequate for what she felt that Katie put her arms entirely around Za in a second big hug. "I'm really going to miss you, Za."

This time Za didn't step out of her embrace. He hugged her back as hard as he could, wrapping his arms around her waist, which was as high as he could reach, and said, "Not for long. As soon as I finish the rest of my initiation, I'm going to study with the native grandparents on Stella. They are the ones with the longest roots who have guarded the old ways of balance on our planet. They'll know how to care for the soil," he said and his yellow eyes lit up with excitement. "Once I've learned enough, I'm going to apply for a permit to work on Earth to help heal the soils on your world." He flashed his adorable blue grin.

Katie smiled, realizing how much she looked forward to Za's visit. It would be fun to introduce her alien friend to her parents and friends. Then she shivered. *What if using the Poison One doesn't work, and we never make it home?* But, she didn't speak her fear aloud. Instead, she said, "Goodbye, Za. Say hello to your guardian for me."

"I will," replied Za, settling himself on Eek's gelatinous back. "I can't wait to tell him we contained the Poison One. That's way beyond what's expected on a journey quest."

Eek shot into the sky before Katie had a chance to answer.

"Quickly!" urged Wind. "We have to follow right behind them so that the Poison One can energize both of us."

"What do I do with the Poison One?" she asked, carefully picking the woven cloth back up from the ground.

"You must hold on to it as we travel between worlds," replied Wind. "The Poison One's trapped energy will be released as we push to the edges of this world's gravity. That should provide enough of a boost to get us through the space between worlds. No matter what happens, don't drop it!"

Katie looked at the small bundle she clutched. Sickening goo peeked out between the glowing hairs.

Wind knelt in her usual style and waited for Katie to mount. When Katie was settled in the warm hollow of Wind's back, the horse flew into the sky. Katie felt Wind's emotions: effort and worry mixed with concern. Then the soothing rocking warmth lulled her into a relaxed state and her mind filled with images of leafy green, of trees whispering in wind, of the scent of pine, of branches lifting them into the heavens.

They shot up and up, at last losing the fragrance of the trees as they passed this world's atmosphere. Katie was aware of planets whirling in their orbits, of moons circling the planets, and meteors streaking past in a complicated ballet. Wind's comforting warmth surrounded her like a blanket. "Just hold on, human child. We haven't long now. Isn't the view lovely?"

It was. Katie looked around with delight, whirling through outer space as if in a dream of beauty: the sequined lights of twinkling stars against the blue-black fabric of the heavens. She listened to a hum that she somehow knew was part of the music of the spheres. So many planets and stars and particles of existence, each with a unique note, and yet it all came together in this incredible beauty that formed a gorgeous net of light so very like the song weave in the earth. Katie realized she could hear only a small fragment of the complex intertwined melody. And yet it seemed to inform her, so that she knew her own small song was somehow related, somehow a fractal of the whole, a small refrain.

The music of her heart drew her in. So many notes! Each one of her moods, each part of her personality, from hot tempered and full of self-doubt to imaginative, kind and able to hear so much, was reflected in the song of her heart and that song was a reflection of the great cosmic symphony.

Her knees gripped tight around Wind as she continued to listen. Her heart was full of joy. *I'm going home!* The image of Sasha, the way she'd seen her when she looked through the gate, came into her mind. *My disappearance probably made things even worse at home.*

"Yes, it did," the Poison One's Voice whispered in her mind. It was faint and feeble, but the words it said struck.

"Your parents are still mad at you. They don't want you back. Not after the way you behaved."

Hot needles bit into Katie's left hand so she could no longer feel it clutching the woven bundle. Fumes of toxic gas leaked out, enveloping her. Katie gasped, choking. She felt dizzy, disoriented and could no longer sense Wind's thoughts at all. She could no longer hear the song of the stars, no longer hear the song in her own heart. Instead it was only the Poison One she could hear saying, "Let me go! Let me go!"

Katie gripped the bundle with unfeeling fingers.

She couldn't see, couldn't hear, and couldn't feel. "Let me go, let me go, let me go!"

"I won't listen!" Katie tried to shout, but no sound came out. Her chest squeezed tighter and tighter. Heavy pressure pushed her down, down, into a nowhere place, a small place of non-being.

"Wind!" Katie cried in her mind, but the horse didn't answer.

"That horse was never real," came the insinuating voice, the only thing Katie could hear.

She felt feverish. So hot. Broiling and then the cells of her body seemed to grow further apart, so she could see stars through the skin of her arm, and then her forearm began to evaporate. Katie could no longer feel the horse. *Had there ever been a horse?* She couldn't feel her body. *Did I ever have a body?* She couldn't feel anything except for her hand, which still clutched the bundle containing the Poison One. She couldn't remember why she was not supposed to let it go. She couldn't remember where she was or who she was. *My name. I must have a name.* But no name came to her.

Ghastly laughter erupted around her. The inky fumes thickened, blotting out the stars. "You don't have a name. You've never had a name. You are nothing!"

Nothing. The word echoed over and over in her head, until her mind went blank, and there was nothing left for it to echo in. Emptiness. Sightless, without smell, or taste, or hearing, or even memory.

The last feeling left her fingers and the cloth bundle slipped out of her hand.

CHAPTER TWENTY-FOUR

Just a Name

"Please come back to us, honey. Please come back, Katie." *Katie*. The word didn't mean anything. *But it should mean something.*

A lovely and well-known voice spoke in her mind, "We barely made it, human child. Fortunately you didn't drop the Poison One until we were nearly here. I had quite a time materializing us after you dropped it! We were almost lost in the void..."

Poison One?

"Don't worry," came the satisfied thought. "Now it's the Poison One who is lost in the void."

Something pressed against her chest. Heavy, soft, purring. "Kira?" she asked, opening her eyes.

A small ginger-colored cat stared back at her with clear green eyes. "Sasha!" exclaimed Katie, sitting up slightly and stroking the cat. "Oh Sasha, is it really you?"

"Honey, she's awake. Katie's awake!" exclaimed Mom.

Dad's dark chocolate eyes beamed down at her. "Welcome back Rosa, my darling precious rose."

Blinking to clear her blurry eyes, Katie gazed up at her parents, joy filling her heart. She'd made it home again!

Wiping the sleep from the corners of her eyes, Katie smiled at Mom. And then she frowned. Mom had a faded red welt on her cheek. The welt *she'd* given her. Katie swallowed around the lump in her throat as the whole fight came back to her. "Mom…Dad. I'm sorry."

"Thank you, sweetheart," said Mom, smoothing Katie's forehead.

Katie looked down at her lavender comforter and said so softly it was almost a whisper, "I should never have thrown my brush. I didn't think it would actually hit you—and certainly not in the face!"

Dad cleared his throat. "I'm sure you've learned your lesson about throwing things," he said, kissing her forehead. "None of us is perfect. I also want to apologize for all the fighting and arguing." He smiled a little sheepishly.

Mom chimed in, "I'm sorry too, Katie. The important thing is that you're better."

"Better?"

"Don't you remember, honey?" asked Mom, straightening Katie's comforter. "You were in the hospital. Between the gas fumes and the concussion, you've lost two whole weeks."

Two weeks? Katie ran her fingers through her hair, noticing that her braid was gone. Instead, someone—probably Mom—had brushed her hair and tied it back into a loose pony tail.

The doorbell rang. "That's probably Amy," said Dad.

Mom called, "Come in!"

A minute later, Amy bounded into the room, tossing her red hair out of her face and saying breathlessly, "I'm so glad you're well." She took her favorite violet sweater off and placed it on the old wooden desk along with her school bag. "Next time you tell me your cat is talking to you, I'm going to believe you! If we'd listened, you would have gotten out of the house in time." Amy gave her a sincere look. "I was so scared you were gone forever and I felt so bad." Tears glistened in Amy's green eyes, making them look almost as emerald as those of the dragon.

"It's okay, Amy," replied Katie, happy to see her friend.

"I told the kids at school you knew the cat was trying to warn us about the quake. Mr. Pinski said that animals do know in advance and that you might also have a way of knowing."

"He did?" asked Katie, amazed.

"Yes," said Amy, handing her a large envelope.

Katie peeked inside and then grinned. The envelope was full of hand drawn get well cards from her whole class. Right on top was an invitation to Maggie's birthday party. Katie showed it to Amy. "Should we go?"

"Maggie was pretty mean," said Amy, holding up a shiny red apple, "but she gave me this for your horse."

"Horse?!" asked Katie, giving her mother a questioning look. This was beyond belief. She pinched herself to be sure she was here. She had to still be dreaming, or lost in some other world. Looking around, Katie half expected to see someone small and short. She could almost picture him, a vague, dreamy figure with big feet. Who was he? But it was her mother gazing down at her and it was her mother's familiar musical voice that spoke. At first Mom's words faded in and out so Katie had to concentrate on listening.

"It was the most peculiar thing," continued Mom. "The day after your injury, there was a sudden big wind and all the chimes rang the most beautiful song and we noticed this horse in the front yard, right in front of the garden. We advertised everywhere, even on local radio and TV, but no one claimed her." Mom raised her eyebrows, obviously still mystified. "She's really been no problem. Calm and quiet, nibbling on grass. Amy has come over every day after school to give her oats and water. So far she seems perfectly content. Hasn't tried to run off or anything."

Katie was all the way awake now. She could not believe her ears. "There really truly is a horse outside?"

"I'll go bring the horse around to the front yard so Katie can see her out the window," Amy volunteered eagerly.

"Great," said Dad, offering his arm to help Katie out of bed. She leaned against the window ledge, making the charm bracelet on her wrist tinkle. She stared down at Seidon's Santa Claus face. Had they given her this at the hospital? Weird she'd dreamt of the fish-man, and here he was on her charm bracelet.

Dad and Mom stood on either side of her. Gasping, Dad pointed. "What?!"

Before their eyes, poppies unfurled, blooming in a blaze of red and orange across the yard. Bees buzzed busily, drinking pollen. Pink azaleas, sweet white alyssum, dandelions and small white daisies adorned the earth. Butterflies followed close behind: yellow and brown swallowtails and monarchs with wings so patterned they reminded Katie of stained glass. Hummingbirds sipped nectar from trellised jasmine and honeysuckle, their jewel-like iridescent blue-green bodies glinting in the sun. "I've never seen anything like this!" exclaimed Mom.

Katie remembered the fairy meadow and the roses and tulips bursting with life and color.

"Are you strong enough to go outside, Katie?" asked Dad, "I have to see what's happening."

Katie nodded her head eagerly.

A bit wobbly on her feet, Katie and the family made their way outside. The old wood floors creaked as they went down the hall and passed the plywood nailed down over the crack she'd fallen through. They walked slowly out the front door onto the porch. Katie's jaw dropped as she gaped, unbelieving, at the blossoming yard. Dad held her elbow as she took the few steps down from the porch and onto the stone path. On the south side of the path, the poppies grew right up to the pond. On the north side, they reached to the slope where Dad's forest garden began. Amy was standing in front of the garden beside a beautiful grey mare.

"She's beautiful," said Katie, reaching out a hand to stroke the sleek neck of the grey horse. Where had she seen a horse like this?

"Isn't she amazing?!" asked Amy, her eyes shining.

"Amazing," said Katie, trying to think. "She reminds me of…" Katie stared at the mare's sides. Tucked smoothly against her silver-grey flank were nearly invisible, translucent wings. "Wind?"

"Of course I am Wind," the golden thought slipped into Katie's mind. "That *is* my name after all."

Katie threw her arms around Wind's neck, burying her face in the mare's mane and noticing the way the opalescent hair sparkled colors, like the ones seen in a soap bubble. Suddenly the whole adventure came flooding back to her, from meeting Za and Dania, to flying through the stars on the back of this beautiful horse. "Wind!" she exclaimed again, too full of joy at completing the quest to say more. "Oh, Wind!"

Mom's forehead furrowed in a puzzled frown.

Katie smiled at her mom. "The horse's name is Wind."

Mom looked even more confused. "You've met her before?"

But Katie didn't have a chance to reply before Dad exclaimed, "Look!" He pointed towards his forest garden.

Mint, chamomile and Saint John's wort grew on the edge of the forest, bordering healthy green carrot tops. Grapes ripened on staked vines. Plump blueberries smothered shrubs, and the dwarf apple tree hung with fruit. Luscious golden pears dangled invitingly. Side by side with Amy and Wind, Katie followed her parents into the forest. Spread out on the forest floor beneath the canopy were huge heads of lettuce, spinach, and chard along with little rings of fluted golden chanterelle mushrooms.

Mom threw her arms around Dad. "It is possible! This is incredible! Why, it's pure magic."

Dad hugged her back. "With a forest garden like this, I can apply for that job to teach biodynamic gardening at the college."

"The Poison One was wrong!" Katie exclaimed happily. "You *will* have help."

Dad raised his eyebrows in a question, "The Poison One?"

"There's no poison here," said Mom, bursting into one of their favorite songs.

'Everything's gonna be alright
If I keep my head to the sky
Everything's gonna be alright'

KATIE, DAD AND AMY SANG ALONG, "EVERYTHING'S gonna be alright." A yellow and green bull frog jumped out of the poppies and croaked along with them.

When they finally stopped singing, Dad smiled his silly ear to ear grin, and Mom laughed. Then they all started laughing and laughing until Katie's belly hurt. Wind whinnied.

Amy stroked the horse's shoulder and whispered, "Are those wings?"

"I'll tell you all about it later." Katie smiled a secret smile, thinking how astonished Amy was going to be when she told her about Za and their adventures. Then she looked at Mom and Dad. "Can I keep Wind?"

"We're not going to say no to your miracle, honey," answered Mom.

And then, both together, Mom and Dad chorused, "Yes!"